PARTNERS

As spring deepened and the weather grew warmer, Davy and Maxi were inseparable. They took little trips to Disneyland and other places; they spent long, quiet hours talking; they went to drive-in movies, skating rinks; they hiked on the beach; they made love in the camper. And everywhere they went, they took their third partner—the bottle. . . .

They tried dozens of hangover remedies. They tried sticking to one kind of booze; they tried drinking and eating together; but they still suffered hangovers. And if they forgot to eat regularly, they never forgot to drink. . . .

(The National Institute on Alcoholism estimates that one million high school kids [1 in 20] get drunk on the average of once a week.)

"Much like GO ASK ALICE . . . "
—NEW YORK TIMES

Bestselling SIGNET VISTA Books

- [ ] **FIRST STEP by Anne Snyder.** Her mother's drinking problem was ruining Cindy's life—or was she ruining things for herself. . . ? A novel about taking that all-important first step. (#W8194—$1.50)

- [ ] **MY NAME IS DAVY—I'M AN ALCOHOLIC by Anne Snyder.** He didn't have a friend in the world—until he discovered booze and Maxi. And suddenly the two of them were in trouble they couldn't handle, the most desperate trouble of their lives. . . . (#Y7978—$1.25)

- [ ] **I NEVER PROMISED YOU A ROSE GARDEN by Joanne Greenberg.** A triumphant film starring Bibi Anderson and Kathleen Quinlan based on the 5,000,000 copy bestseller. An extraordinary story about a sixteen-year-old girl who hid from life in the seductive world of madness. (#J9700—$2.25)

- [ ] **I WANT TO KEEP MY BABY! by Joanne Lee.** Based on the emotion-packed CBS Television Special starring Mariel Hemingway, about a teenage girl in grown-up trouble. The most emotion-wrenching experience you will ever live through . . . "It will move you, touch you, give you something to think about."—*Seattle Times* (#E9884—$1.75)

- [ ] **MARY JANE HARPER CRIED LAST NIGHT by Joanne Lee and T. S. Cook.** Here is a deeply moving novel and sensational CBS TV movie that brings the full horror of child abuse home. A rich, spoiled, and emotionally disturbed young mother, abandoned by her husband, takes her frustration out on her little girl . . . "Powerful, riveting, stinging, revealing!"—*Hollywood Reporter* (#E9692—$1.75)

Buy them at your local bookstore or use this convenient coupon for ordering.

THE NEW AMERICAN LIBRARY, INC.,
P.O. Box 999, Bergenfield, New Jersey 07621

Please send me the books I have checked above. I am enclosing $_____
(please add $1.00 to this order to cover postage and handling). Send check or money order—no cash or C.O.D.'s. Prices and numbers are subject to change without notice.

Name_____

Address_____

City _____ State _____ Zip Code _____
Allow 4-6 weeks for delivery.
This offer is subject to withdrawal without notice.

MY NAME IS DAVY
I'm an Alcoholic

by

Anne Snyder

A SIGNET VISTA BOOK

NEW AMERICAN LIBRARY

TIMES MIRROR

For my beloved daughters,
Sherri, Mari-beth, and Nathalie.

1

The alarm clock had been ringing steadily for a while now. Finally, without opening his eyes, Davy reached out and shut the clanging off. He rolled over and sat up groggily on the edge of the bed. Elbows on his knees, he held his head in his hands and gently massaged his scalp.

There was a knock on the door. "Davy, are you up? Time for school."

"I'm up, I'm up," mumbled Davy.

"Breakfast is ready."

Davy sighed. "Coming," he said. He could hear his mother move away from the door.

He was feeling rotten. A nagging pain gnawed at the back of his head and his entire body shook. He held out his hands and tried to steady them. They were trembling like an old man's.

He got up and headed for the closet. Just one to get me started, he thought. He had promised himself that he would quit today. And he now promised himself again that he would—right after lunch. What difference did a few hours make?

He stepped into the walk-in closet, switched on the light, and shut the door. He reached back into the pocket of a heavy jacket and brought out a bottle. He stared at the liquor in his hand. No, he thought, I'm quitting—once and for all. He shoved the bottle back into the pocket and, feeling pleased with himself, left the closet.

In the shower, Davy wondered how he'd make it through the day. His first class was English. He could fake his way through that one. They were "doing" *Hamlet*. Davy had loved the play ever since he read it when he was still in junior high. Why did the teacher have to go and spoil the whole thing for him by tearing it apart, analyzing it down to its bones, talking the life out of it?

Today they were supposed to tell the meaning of the play in one lousy sentence. As far as he was concerned the meaning was simply that it's sometimes better to take any kind of action than to get hung up sitting on the fence. But he knew that Miss Cunningham would want something that sounded deeper, more complicated. He remembered reading what some German guy had written about *Hamlet:* "He sinks beneath a burden which he cannot bear, and cannot cast aside." Miss Cunningham would go for that. He'd lay that one on her.

Davy stepped out of the shower and reached for the terry-cloth towel. Second class, typing. That class was a bummer. All that clattering, his headache was sure to get worse. Well, he'd sweat it out somehow. Then, phys—ed. Davy groaned. Maybe he could skip it. He shook his head. No way. He'd done that yesterday and Coach Scully had ripped into him again.

He thought, as he combed his hair, how he'd like to chuck it all. He'd be sixteen soon. He could quit school, drop out, get a job. What could his parents do, kill him?

He ran a trembling hand over his hair, then opened the medicine cabinet and looked hard at a brown bottle labeled Cough Syrup. He had filled the bottle with scotch last night. One drink would stop the shakes. But he told himself he was quitting, and he angrily slammed the door shut and finished his dressing.

In the kitchen, his mother was pouring milk into his thermos. "Better hurry, you're late," she said.

Davy grunted a greeting, poured himself a cup of coffee, and sat down at the table.

"Eggs?" asked his mother.

"No thanks."

"How about cereal?"

"Not hungry."

"You've got to eat something." His mother took a cup of coffee and sat down opposite him.

3

"I don't know what you're living on these days," she said.

Davy gulped down his coffee and pushed the mug aside. He picked up his lunch bag and started for the door.

"Davy," she called after him, "dinner will be in the oven for you tonight. I'll be at class."

Davy turned and nodded. He'd never get used to his mother taking classes—a woman over fifty going to school.

"But I'll make it up to you tomorrow night," she said. "Your father will be home. We'll have a good dinner."

"Sure," said Davy. He started for the front door but couldn't get past the den. The wet bar was in there. And all he could think of were the bottles. He could see them all lined up in a row. The picture would not leave his mind. He hated himself as he opened the door and ducked inside. But why should he feel guilty? He told himself to go easy on himself, stop putting himself down. He had promised himself to quit drinking, and he intended to keep his promise after lunch. For now, he stood at the bar and poured milk from his thermos into the sink. Then he filled the thermos with scotch, making a mental note to replace the whiskey before his dad came home tomorrow night. As he turned to go, he took a deep swallow from the scotch bottle and shuddered.

As Davy walked up to the school, he kept his eye out for the old blue van. The fantasy began again, as it did every morning. He saw himself greeting the kids in the van in a friendly way. Then he'd get Linda Harper aside. "Hi, Linda, how's it going?" he'd say.

"Fine," she'd answer. "How about you?"

"Terrific, couldn't be better. Say, Linda, how about a movie tonight?"

"Sure," she'd smile. "Pick me up at seven-thirty." Then she'd take his hand and squeeze it. "Don't keep me waiting."

The beat-up blue van pulled up at the curb and a bunch of kids came spilling out. Linda and Mike, the driver, sat inside for a moment and talked. When they joined the kids on the sidewalk. Maxine Chudler made a beeline for Linda and took her arm possessively.

Davy's heart began to pound at the sight of Linda. Her honey-colored hair hung straight and shining down her back, and her perfect figure, outlined by her too-tight jeans, was unreal. She laughed at something Mike whispered in her ear. Mike was where the fun was. He had it all together—handsome, popular, daring. Davy heard that he was even busted once but had gotten off with a warning. Linda glanced up. Davy thought she looked at him. He stopped walking, he stopped breathing. He waved at her. But she didn't see him; she turned back to Mike.

5

As he passed the group of kids, Davy could hear them laughing. Were they laughing at him? Naw, they didn't even know he was alive ... least of all, Linda.

A wave of guilt swept over him as he remembered his fantasies about her. Night after night, Davy day-dreamed about Linda: Linda naked, Linda in his arms, in his bed, kissing Linda, fondling Linda, touching her breasts, doing it to her. If she knew what he thought, she'd probably hate his guts.

Maybe tomorrow. Tomorrow, he'd speak to her. He'd go right up and kind of casually greet the kids ... ahh hell, he knew he wouldn't do it. Who was he trying to kid? Even if he ever did get the nerve, they'd probably tell him to buzz off. Why'd they want to bother with him, a real nobody?

Well, he didn't need them. He didn't need anyone.

In the school, the tinny crash of slamming lockers rang in his ears as he walked down the hall. The noise aggravated the nagging pain at the back of his head.

His locker was next to Mike's. He'd put his stuff away and split before Mike and Linda got there. The pain of being ignored overshadowed his desire to catch another glimpse of Linda.

Davy hung his sweater on the hook. His head ached in earnest, and he felt a dull throbbing over one eye. He reached into his lunch bag, opened the thermos, and took a quick swallow. As he did so, he hit his elbow and the fluid splashed out of the bottle. He turned to find himself face to face with Mike, Linda at his side. Davy's eyes were riveted on the dark, wet stain on the front of Mike's T-shirt where some of the scotch had spurted.

Mike looked at his shirt in annoyance. Then he sniffed broadly and rolled his eyes upward. "What have we here?" he said. He passed a finger over the stain and stuck it in his mouth. "Contraband!" he exclaimed.

Davy froze.

"What is it?" asked Linda.

"Nectar of the gods," Mike stage-whispered. "Booze."

Linda stared at Davy unbelievingly. He tried to put the thermos away, but Mike quickly reached out and snatched it from him.

"Share the wealth, kid. This is a democracy," Mike laughed. He took a sip from the thermos and passed it to Linda. She tipped the bottle and gave it back to Davy.

"Still water runs deep, as my sainted grandmother always said," Mike kidded. "Imagine little Davy Kimble sitting on top of an oil well and keeping it to himself all this time."

"Wonder what other interesting secrets he's got," laughed Linda.

7

"Let's find out," said Mike. "Where do you hang out at lunchtime?"

"Cafeteria," mumbled Davy.

"More action under the bleachers. Meet us there, okay?"

Davy looked at him, then at Linda. She smiled.

"Twelve o'clock. We'll be waiting for you," she said.

Davy couldn't believe his ears. "What? Sure, okay," he stammered.

"And bring the liquid gold," said Mike.

Davy grinned. "I'll be there," he said.

At lunchtime when Davy arrived at the bleachers, the guys and girls were not overly friendly at first. But soon it was like a real party, and Davy and his trusty thermos were the hit of the day. Mike kept referring to him as "my friend, the swinger." And Linda possessively took his arm and warned Maxine, kiddingly, "Hands off Davy, I saw him first."

Still, Davy felt on the outside looking in, like a stranger.

Mike had a joint which he passed around, and Maxine pumped vodka into oranges with a hypodermic needle. Everyone laughed as she plunged the needle into orange after orange. Not much booze got into the fruit, but Davy cracked up watching the gleeful look of the kids sucking on those innocent-looking oranges.

8

Before they parted, Linda told Davy the gang would be cruising the boulevard that night. "We'll be passing Van Nuys Boulevard and Victory about eightish," she said. "I'll be looking for you."

Davy's feet hardly touched the ground as he walked home after school. He thought about how the group had accepted him; well, if they hadn't exactly accepted him, they hadn't rejected him either. This was the clique he'd always envied, the group known as the "rowdies," the ones who seemed to be having the most fun. If he'd had a choice of belonging to one group or another at school, he'd have chosen these kids; they seemed the most adult. But he belonged to no group. He certainly was no scholar; he wasn't part of the "bitchin" bunch, the stuck-up group; and he had only contempt for the others—the ones who were straight like himself. There wasn't even a particular person, a special friend he hung around with. He was no place. But now things were different. He'd be cruising tonight. He'd be seeing Linda.

Suddenly, he grew worried. What would he do when he got there? What would he talk about? He wasn't witty like Mike or funny like Cliff or tough like Paul. He was an outsider—he didn't belong . . . he'd never belong.

A wave of fear gripped him, the inexplicable

anxiety with which he constantly lived—a feeling of impending doom. His skin felt clammy and his lips were dry. What he needed was a good, stiff drink. But there was none. After passing his thermos around at lunchtime, there hadn't been anything left in it for him. He hadn't had a drink since early in the morning—or anything to eat, either.

Well, he'd eat something, take a long, hot bath, and crash for a couple of hours. By tonight, he'd be in good shape.

At home, he stopped at the doorway of the den. He needed a drink, but he thought of Linda and made himself pass it up. He wanted to be sharp for her tonight. He went on to the kitchen.

On the kitchen table, he found a note: *Davy, meat loaf in oven, salad in refrig. Late class tonight. See you in* A.M. *Mom.*

Forcing down some meat loaf and a glass of milk, Davy thought of his mother. Taking all those college courses. Art, comparative religion, anthropology. Not that she was going to school for a degree or anything like that. She had to keep busy, she said, keep her mind occupied so she wouldn't have to think. He shook his head. His mother; practically a senior citizen, going to school where you *had* to think, just to *keep* from thinking. It didn't make sense.

In the bathroom, Davy lowered himself into the tub and leaned back. The water was warm and relaxing. With his toes, he turned the hot water faucet on to a trickle so his bath wouldn't cool off. Boy, all he needed now, to make things perfect, would be a swift drink from that bottle in the medicine cabinet. No. Better not think of that. Think of something else. Like Mother does. But an image of the bottle labeled Cough Syrup kept plaguing him. Shit, it seemed he'd been thinking of nothing but booze all his life. What had he thought about before he started to drink?

Davy closed his eyes and remembered himself as a small boy. His parents were middle-aged by the time he was born, and he was always with adults. He was like a miniature old man. The only thing he liked about himself was that he always loved to read. But he wouldn't just read the books he got at the library on Saturdays, he'd attack them. It was like he'd get on a "book binge" and couldn't stop reading even if he wanted to. And he had a thing about never mixing his reading. He read anything; *Tarzan of the Apes*, science fiction, horror stories, anything. But only one kind of thing at a time. And he always had to finish a book, even if he hated it. It was that way with movies and TV, too. Once he started a thing, he couldn't seem to stop. Like drinking.

He remembered the first time he ever drank.

It was New Year's Eve, and his parents had gone out. Oh, he had tasted his parents' cocktails before, but he had never had a whole drink to himself.

He was sitting in the den in front of the television set watching the celebrations from all over the country, but his mind wasn't on the show. He was thinking about how all the kids he knew had someplace to go that night. Even the nobodies were having parties of their own. He must be the only kid in the world who had to sit around alone on New Year's Eve, he thought dismally.

Davy had switched the TV set to another channel. It showed a bunch of kids dancing to some hard rock music. He changed the channel again. The scene was of a party in progress, the people holding champagne glasses and singing around a piano. In a close shot, one man held up his glass and toasted the new year. Then everyone broke into "Auld Lang Syne."

Gloomily, Davy had watched the festivities on the TV set. Then he thought of the stock of liquor in the bar behind him and he went and poured some whiskey into a water glass. Bringing the glass with him, he sat down and toasted the singing figures on the TV screen. He took a stiff drink. His eyes watered as he choked and gagged. He took another sip, this time a small one. He sang along with the TV and finished off the drink. It went down easier this time. His depression lifted.

He had filled his glass again and drunk up. He began to feel warm and glowing, almost happy. He was suddenly as cool as, as tall as, as tough as anyone.

After that evening, he took a drink whenever he felt down. He found that when he drank he was comfortable with himself. Drinking made the rough edges smooth, made him feel like part of the human race; it smothered the hollow, empty loneliness.

And ever since that New Year's Eve, more than a year ago, he had been drinking secretly—and steadily.

Davy turned the hot water off with his toe. He scrunched down in the water and sighed. He thought about Linda, about making love to her. Linda . . . Linda.

Guiltily, Davy got out of the tub. If he wanted to be at his best tonight, he'd better cut out the dirty thoughts and go take a nap.

A sense of excitement filled Davy as he walked down the boulevard that evening. The streets were overflowing. There were kids in cars; kids on motorcycles; kids perched on the roofs of parked vehicles; herds of kids just standing around or lounging on the lawn of a funeral parlor; kids crowding into coffee shops and around hot dog stands; and kids careening up and down the boulevard in customized, souped-up cars.

Davy looked after a Model T sounding its ancient horn: "oogah, oogah, oogah!" Another car joined in, clamoring the first bars of "How Dry I Am." More horns got into the act until the air was filled with beepings and honkings. He laughed at the crazy carnival atmosphere.

On the sidewalk, some chanting Hare Krishna kids handed him a pamphlet. Here, at the corner of Van Nuys Boulevard and Victory, he glanced at his watch. Seven-thirty. Plenty of time. Linda had said eightish.

To kill time, Davy fooled around at the newsstand along with some other kids who were smirking at the pornographic newspapers and magazines. Then he looked at his watch again and went to stand beside the signal light. He didn't want to miss Linda.

Three girls walked by, all looking alike with their long, straight hair and washed-out jeans. A purple sports car full of boys slowed down and a guy stuck his head out the window and yelled. "Want a lift, chicks?"

"Get lost, creep!" shouted one of the girls. They giggled as they went on.

Inside a passing surf-wagon, Davy thought he saw Linda. His heart leaped, but when the girl turned, it was someone else.

"Hey, jock!" the stranger called. "Need a ride?"

14

Davy smiled and shook his head.

"See ya!" she yelled as the car peeled out.

An open pickup truck stopped for a red light. The truckbed was packed with kids singing:

> *A hundred bottles of beer on the wall,*
> *A hundred bottles of beer . . .*

They sang at the top of their lungs. A girl inside held up a can of Coke as if to toast Davy.

> *Through the teeth,*
> *Over the gums,*
> *Look out, stomach,*
> *Here it comes!*

she shouted over the torqued engine, and threw an unopened can at Davy. He caught it as the pickup drove off, and stuck it in his jacket pocket.

One of the police cars which were always cruising the boulevard busting kids for possession, drunk driving, or just for loitering slowed down to look him over.

A store manager stepped into his doorway and gave Davy a dirty look. The merchants hated the kids; the cruising hurt business. But the police couldn't stop the cruising or the congregation of kids on Van Nuys Boulevard on a Wednesday night. It had been going on for ages. Davy thought of the kid at school whose parents had met on the boulevard, and who was now a cruiser himself.

Davy looked at his watch again. Eight-fifteen. Where was Linda? Had he missed her? As he thought about it he realized that she hadn't actually invited him to be there. All she had said was that she'd be looking for him. Maybe she wasn't coming. He should have known it would turn out like this. She wouldn't show—the evening would be a bust. He decided to wait another fifteen minutes, then go home.

Soon, Mike's familiar dirty blue van pulled up to the curb. "Hey, Davy!" Mike yelled.

"Hi," answered Davy.

"What you carrying?"

Davy had forgotten about the Coke in his bulging pocket. "Nothing . . . it's nothing."

Mike laughed. "Hop in."

Paul, in the passenger seat, flung open the door.

"I was sort of waiting around," said Davy.

"Get in," said Paul. "The cops are across the street. Come on."

Davy glanced at the California Highway Patrol car on the other side of the boulevard. One of the cops was looking straight at him.

As he scrambled into the van, he was hit by the strong smell of booze. He looked over his shoulder. Cliff and Stan were in the back sitting on a mattress. But Linda was not there.

2

As the old blue van rumbled and wheezed down the street, Davy felt a pang of disappointment. Linda, his reason for coming, wasn't around.

Paul tapped Davy's bulging pocket. "What you got good, man?"

"Nothing but a Coke," said Davy.

"Kid stuff," groaned Paul.

So that's why they picked me up, thought Davy. They thought I had booze. Now, they'll probably dump me at the next street corner.

"Joke's on us," laughed Mike. "Ah well, give the new man a real drink."

"Better hurry and catch up," Paul said, "we're way ahead of you."

"That's okay, I can drink Coke," Davy said, popping open the can.

"We're extremely magnanimous fellows," said Mike, waving a hand. "On us."

Davy was confused. Were the guys really being friendly or were they putting him on?

17

Paul, tall, powerful, clumsily built, handed Davy a McDonald's paper cup with bourbon in it. "Don't be so straight, have some real stuff. Go on, drink up."

Davy hesitated, then: Well, why not? he thought. I'll quit tomorrow. He poured some bourbon into the paper cup and downed the drink in one gulp, savoring the familiar, warm burning sensation.

"Wow!" marveled Paul. "That man drinks like a man!"

Davy grinned at Paul. It's all right, he thought. They like me. They're great guys.

"How about passing the stuff back here?" said Cliff from behind. "We're fresh out."

"Coming up," said Paul. He poured another drink into Davy's cup, then gave the bottle to Cliff. Cliff filled his cup and passed the bottle to Stan.

The van stopped for a red light. A yellow convertible, full of girls, pulled up in the lane beside them. They were the classiest clique in school.

"Check out the chicks," said Mike.

"Lemme at 'em!" Paul bellowed. He crawled over Davy and hung his head out the window. "Wanna have a party?" he yelled.

"Get lost!" said the pretty driver.

"Hey, Paul, shoot the moon," said Cliff. Go on, hang a bare-ass!"

"Yeah, show 'em your better side," said Stan.

18

"Okay, keep up with them," Paul said to Mike. "I'll crack them a smile!"

Mike chuckled. "Right on!" he said, gunning the motor.

Davy had heard of hanging a bare-ass but he'd never seen one done. He finished off his drink and watched. Paul rolled up the window, unbuckled his belt, and let his pants down.

At the next light, both cars stopped. Mike blasted his horn for the girls' attention as Paul pulled down his shorts and pressed his naked buttocks against the window. The boys hooted and howled. Davy laughed, too, but couldn't help feeling a twinge of embarrassment.

Pretending hard not to notice, the girl at the wheel stared straight ahead, while the others laughed and snickered. The B.A. was a huge success.

When the light changed, the yellow convertible sped across the intersection, leaving the van stuck behind a car making a left turn.

Paul pulled up his pants, then took an unopened bottle out of the glove compartment. "That calls for another drink all around," he said. He opened the bottle and began filling paper cups.

"I wouldn't throw that little redhead in the back seat out of bed for eating crackers," said Cliff, reaching for his drink. "Just give me fifteen minutes with her."

19

"Why be discriminating?" said Mike. "I'd take any of them—or all of them."

"Me, I'd take the blonde driving the car," said Paul. "How about you, Davy?"

Davy felt himself blushing. "I don't know . . . I guess I like blondes." Honey-blondes, he thought, like Linda.

"Hey," said Stan over Davy's shoulder, "I'll bet little Davy here has never even had a piece yet."

Davy was hit with a sinking feeling. The guys were putting him on, making fun of him. He should have known.

"How about it, Davy, have you?" said Paul.

Davy took a swallow from his cup. "Well, not exactly."

"Close, but no cigar," laughed Cliff.

"It's an *exact* science—you did or you didn't," sniggered Paul.

"If he did, he'd remember—exactly," said Mike. "Poor guy, doesn't know what he's missing."

"We'll have to fix that someday," said Cliff. "Davy's our friend, isn't he?"

"Sure," said Paul. "Gotta fix Davy up someday."

"Wait a minute, I got an idea," said Mike. "We'll fix Davy up tonight, now."

"That's all right," said Davy. "Don't bother."

"Like I said, Davy, we're very magmanimous . . . magnaminous . . . we're very generous. We'll treat good ole Davy to his first lay, his first horizontal rumba, okay, guys?"

The boys agreed with catcalls and howls.

Davy was miserable. He was sorry about the morning, sorry about the afternoon, sorry about everything.

"Who'll we get?" asked Paul.

"Gotta get someone we can count on," Mike said, slurring his words.

"How about Ellen?" said Cliff.

"Naw," said Stan. "She's Ted's old lady."

Davy squirmed in the silence as the boys tried to think of a likely candidate for him.

Then Mike smacked the heel of his hand to his forehead. "I know," he said. "And she's got a place of her own."

"Who?" asked Paul.

"Maxine . . . good old Maxi's got a camper."

"How do you know she'll give?" asked Stan.

"She's a sport . . . good old Maxi's everybody's pal," said Mike.

"Onward to Maxi's place!" whooped Cliff. He broke into song as Mike turned the van off the boulevard, the others joining in:

Oh, he jumped in bed and covered up his head,
And said she couldn't find him,
But she knew damn well he lied like hell,
And she jumped right in beside him . . .

21

The boys laughed and started another rau-cous, drunken chorus.

Davy wished he could disappear. This wasn't the way he'd planned his first encounter. He'd thought about it often enough. It was going to be love, soft lights, and music . . . and Linda.

The guys ended their song and passed the bottle around. Davy filled his cup to the top and drank. The more he drank, the better he felt. It was too late. He was trapped. He'd have to go along with the guys.

Mike glanced over at Davy. "It'll be great. Don't worry," he said.

"Who's worried?" said Davy.

"Nothing to it," Paul said. "What you don't know. Maxi'll teach you," he snickered.

Mike steered the van down a darkened side street and pulled up in front of a small stucco house. A camper was parked at the back of a narrow driveway, lights shining from its tiny windows. Beside it was Maxi's Camaro. The house itself was dark.

"Think it's all clear?" said Paul.

"Sure," Mike answered. "Her old man doesn't come home until after two." He turned to Davy. "How you doing?"

"I don't feel so good," said Davy. "We could come back tomorrow—some other time."

"The time is now—now or never," Mike said thickly.

22

"I'll give him some more courage," offered Paul, pouring him another drink.

Davy stalled, swallowing the drink, as Mike got out of the van, came to the passenger side, and opened the door. Paul slid out, dragging Davy with him. The two boys held Davy up as they staggered up the driveway to the camper.

Paul knocked on the camper door. "Anyone home?"

"We'll huff and we'll puff and we'll blow your house down," sang Mike.

The door opened. Davy looked dizzily at Maxi outlined in the doorway, the light behind her. "Hey, what is this?" she said. "What are you up to, Mike?"

Davy tried to break away, but the boys held him fast.

"Brought you a pigeon. Take good care of him," said Mike.

"What are you talking about?" said Maxi.

"Brought Davy . . . little virgin . . . needs some lovin'," slurred Paul.

"You're all crazy . . . go home!" said Maxi.

"One-two-three, heave!" said Mike as he and Paul shoved Davy up the step, and through the doorway and ran off to the van.

Davy and Maxi stood facing each other. She seemed to be wavering before him.

She shook her head. "Boy, you really hung

23

one on," she said. "Here, sit down." She led him to the bunk at the side of the camper.

Davy sat down heavily. He could feel the perspiration on his forehead, under his arms.

"Take off your coat, it's warm in here," said Maxi, sitting beside him.

Davy reached out for her but she seemed to be drifting fading away . . . fading . . .

When Davy awakened, Maxi appeared to him through a haze sitting at the foot of the bunk. Even in the dim light, he could see she was naked. He raised himself on one elbow and she turned and smiled at him. Embarrassed, he tried to look away but couldn't drag his eyes off her. He'd seen her before, lots of times, and he had never thought of her as pretty. She was short and a bit too plump. But now she looked beautiful. With the shadow falling over one shoulder and breast like that, she was lovely, like some kind of painting.

"Feeling better?" she said. Her voice seemed blurred and flat.

Davy nodded, unable to speak. He made himself lower his eyes.

Max laughed. "You're cute," she said. She stood up and started to dress. "Come on, we'll have to get out of here before my dad gets home." She threw him his jacket.

Clumsily, Davy put his jacket on. His head

swam. What had happened? Did he get it on with her? "Maxi?"

"Yeah?"

How could he ask her? Geeze, how do you ask a girl whether you did it to her or not?

She looked at him, "Yeah, Davy?"

"What time is it?" he said finally.

"A little after two. Let's go. I'll drive you home."

As Maxi pulled the Camaro out of the driveway, another car drew up in front of the house. "Damn, it's my dad," she said.

A tall man got out of the car. "Maxi!" he shouted, but she sped away, pretending not to hear him.

"You going to get in trouble?" asked Davy, concerned.

Maxi sighed. "I don't know. Most times he comes home loaded. He may be dead asleep by the time I get back."

"Turn right, here," said Davy. He glanced at her as she made the turn. Her dark, curly hair framed her face. She wasn't a knockout like Linda, but she was kind of pretty in an interesting way.

She was older than he, by at least a year. What was she thinking? Did she think he was a dumb kid, too young to go to bed with a girl? What *did* happen? What a bummer! His first experience, and he couldn't even remember if he did or if he didn't.

25

"I'm sorry," he said.

"What for?"

"I fell asleep . . . I'm sorry."

She chuckled. "No sweat. Forget it."

Except for his giving directions, they were silent the rest of the way home.

When they pulled up to Davy's house, he noticed his father's car in the driveway and the lights on in the house.

"Uh, oh," said Davy.

"What's the matter?"

"My father wasn't supposed to be home until tomorrow night."

"Now, you'll be in trouble," said Maxi. "I'm really sorry."

"Not your fault." He turned to open the door.

"Davy?" He looked at her. "Davy, you're nice. I like you."

Davy smiled. "Good night," he said.

"See ya," said Maxi.

Davy waited until the car drove off, then he took a deep breath and walked up to the house.

His mother met him at the door. "Davy, it's you! Thank God! Davy's home!" she called over her shoulder. "Where have you been? We've been so worried! I was about to call the police!" She paused and looked at him closely. "Oh my God, you've been drinking!"

Davy walked past her and started for his room, but his father's deep voice stopped him.

He could tell his father was in one of his tempers by the sound of his voice. Davy had always been afraid of his dad. He'd often wished his father would hit him rather than go into one of his rages.

Frank Kimble never touched his son—either in affection or in rage. He was a large man with a shock of white, shining hair. At the moment, his face was red with anger. "All right," he said, "where the hell were you?"

Davy grabbed the back of a chair for support. "Out," he said, "just out with the guys."

"This late? On a school night?" said his mother.

"I'll handle this!" his father said.

Davy's stomach rumbled and a wave of nausea washed over him.

"So you were out—out where?" said Frank.

"I feel sick," Davy said. He sat down in the chair.

"You're drunk!" said his father.

"Frank, talk to him in the morning. The boy's sick," Martha said.

"I'll talk to him now!" Frank took a nearly empty bottle of scotch off a table and waved it over Davy's head. "What about this? You took my good liquor, didn't you?"

Davy nodded weakly.

Martha sighed. "At least it's not drugs," she said. "We can be thankful for that."

"This is bad enough," said Frank. "I ought to kick his ass! Fifteen-year-old kid, out half the night, steals my whiskey, comes home drunk!"

"I'll pay for it . . . the liquor . . . there was a party . . ."

"Frank, this is the first time. He's never done it before," said his mother.

Frank put the bottle down and looked at him. "Your mother's right," he said in a calmer tone. "This is the first time—but you'd better not repeat it. I'm warning you." He poured himself a drink and sat down on the chair opposite Davy. "I'm not saying drinking's bad, but first you have to be old enough."

Davy shook his head and swallowed hard. He felt as if there was a glob of warm oil sloshing around in the pit of his stomach.

"It's okay to hoist a few," Frank went on, "but a gentleman knows when he's had enough. Hell, when you're a little older you can drink whenever you want—at home. You won't have to go sneaking out behind our backs." He seemed to be enjoying his pitch. "A little drink never hurt anyone, just so long as it's kept under control. Understand?"

Davy grunted. "Can I go now?"

"Go ahead," said his father. "Get some rest. We can all use a little sleep around here. Just remember what I said."

Davy bolted out of the room and made it to

his bathroom just in time to fall on his knees at the toilet and throw up.

The bed was spinning when he got into it. He held tightly onto the edges of the mattress and let himself be whirled away.

3

Before he opened his eyes, Davy was aware of a rank, sour smell. His tongue felt thick and furry. He opened his mouth to yawn and realized where the stink was coming from. He had to go brush his teeth. An uprush of nausea swept over him as he got unsteadily to his feet.

He glanced at the clock. It was early. Good. He'd get out of the house before his parents were awake. He wasn't in the mood to talk to anyone this morning—or to hear any lectures from his father. He threw off his clothes and put on his robe. Going toward the bathroom, his feet went straight forward but his head was reeling; he walked on a kind of tilt.

He brushed his teeth, then got into the shower and scrubbed vigorously, but he couldn't shake the disconnected feeling between his head and his body. He trembled as he rubbed himself dry.

He took the cough syrup bottle out of the medicine chest and drew a long drink. Feeling better instantly, he sighed and took another swallow. He stood contemplating the bottle. He'd never get through this day without a drink. Taking the bottle with him, he left the bathroom.

Miss Cunningham's voice droned on. Davy looked at his watch. Still fifteen minutes to go before the English class was over. The medicine bottle in his pocket pressed against his thigh like a live thing. He was sick—he needed his medicine, his cough medicine. He cleared his throat loudly.

"I'm going to ask you all to memorize Hamlet's soliloquy," said Miss Cunningham.

The class groaned in unison.

"That'll do," said Miss Cunningham. "You'll have a week to learn it, then we'll have a quiz. Barbara, will you begin reading? Start at the top of the page."

Barbara stood up. " 'To be, or not to be: that is the question . . .' " she began.

Davy coughed.

" 'Whether 'tis nobler in the mind to suffer the slings and arrows . . .' " the girl went on.

Davy's coughing grew louder. He held his hand before his mouth and his face reddened as he choked and sputtered, drowning out Barbara's recitation. The kids tittered and laughed.

"Davy," said Miss Cunningham, "would you like to go see the nurse?"

31

That was the last thing Davy wanted to do. "No, it's all right," he gasped. "I have cough syrup in my pocket. I'll take some after class."

"Take some now, and let's get on with the reading."

"Now?" asked Davy.

"Now," said the teacher.

Well, if she insists, thought Davy ruefully. He pulled the bottle from his pocket and took a sip.

"Continue reading, Barbara," said Miss Cunningham.

The girl read on in a monotone: " 'or to take arms against a sea of troubles, and by opposing end them . . . to die . . . to sleep . . . ' "

Davy closed his eyes. The words wafted over him as a feeling of well-being took over. He dozed.

"Davy!"

Davy started. Miss Cunningham was standing over him.

"Are you sick?"

"I'm fine . . . I'll be fine."

Miss Cunningham sniffed and looked at him closely. "Let's see that bottle."

Davy's heart sank. "It's just cough syrup," he said.

Someone in the class guffawed.

The teacher held her hand out. Davy pulled the bottle out of his pocket and gave it to her. She took off her glasses and read the label.

"Have you read the contents? There's alcohol in this medicine," said Miss Cunningham.

"Oh, yeah?" said Davy innocently.

Fixing him with her eyes, she gave the bottle back to Davy. He looked back at her, staring her down. Finally she sighed and said, "Don't take any more for another four hours."

"I won't, Miss Cunningham," said Davy. He was safe. Either the bottle had fooled her or she didn't want to go to the trouble to make waves.

The bell rang. "Class is dismissed," she said tonelessly.

Davy avoided Mike and the gang at lunchtime. Supposing Maxi had told them what happened last night? Or worse, what didn't happen?

But it was not so easy to keep away from Mike during phys—ed. The class was jogging around the track when Davy noticed Mike coming up behind him. He quickened his pace.

"Hey, Davy . . . wait up."

Davy pretended not to hear. He sprinted ahead with an effort, the sweat pouring down his face.

Mike was at his side. "Trying to break . . . a record?" Davy slowed to a trot. He was out of breath and his mouth was so dry he couldn't swallow.

"How . . . was it?" asked Mike.

33

"How was what?" Davy puffed.

"You know . . . last night . . . Maxi?"

"Oh, that."

"Well?"

"Well . . . what?"

"Come on, man. You know . . . what I'm talking about . . . last night, Maxi? How'd . . . it go?"

"Okay," said Davy breathlessly.

"Yahoo!" Mike shouted. They slowed down at the starting line. Mike thumped Davy on the back. "Congratulations, man!"

The two stopped and stood there puffing and panting. Mike laughed. "You didn't have to be so brutal, though."

"What are you talking about?"

"See Maxi today?"

"No," said Davy.

"Looks like she got in a fight with a tank or something."

"Why? What happened?" asked Davy.

"Beats me," said Mike. He turned away. "Shower, here I come!"

Davy felt a twinge of panic as he watched the older boy go into the locker room. Had Maxi gotten into an accident on the way home? Had she been jumped? It had been pretty late for a girl to be out alone.

Whatever had happened, he felt partly responsible.

The rest of the day dragged on endlessly. When school was over, Davy walked down Cedros Street. He had seen Maxi park the red Camaro there in the past. He spotted the car and waited beside it.

Groups of kids came by, and then he saw Maxi walking alone, wearing huge round sunglasses. When she noticed him, she waved and hurried to the car.

"Hi, Davy," she said.

Davy noticed her swollen lip and could see the discoloration of one of her eyes under the shades.

"What happened?" said Davy.

Maxi shrugged. "Get in the car," she said, unlocking the door. "I'll drive you home."

Maxi lit a cigarette while waiting for Davy to get in. She steered the car into the flow of traffic.

"Cigarette?"

"No thanks," said Davy.

"How are you feeling? Any better?" asked Maxi.

"I'm okay," said Davy. "Just a little hung over."

Maxi laughed, then touched her finger to her lip. "It only hurts when I laugh," she said.

"What'd you do, fall down or something?"

"My old man. He wasn't asleep when I got home."

"Christ," said Davy. He felt sick. It *was* his fault. "Christ," he said again.

Maxi waved a hand. "It's not fatal," she said nonchalantly. "My own fault. Should have started you home a little earlier."

She turned the radio on to a rock music station and tapped the wheel with a finger in time to the music. She glanced at him and smiled crookedly. "Got to go right home?"

"No."

"Why don't we go to my hideout?"

"Your what?"

"My hideout. I go there when I want to be alone."

She sounded like a little kid sharing a childish secret. Davy smiled. "Okay," he said. "Let's go."

"I've never taken anyone there before," she said softly.

Davy laughed. "I'm honored," he said. "Where is it?"

"You'll see," said Maxi.

Listening to the music, they drove along Magnolia Boulevard. Maxi lit another cigarette from the stub of her old one and threw the butt out the window.

Davy leaned back and relaxed. He rolled down the window. It was a beautiful California spring day. The wind was brisk enough to wash off the smog, and the crevices in the mountains could be seen clearly in the distance.

Maxi stopped the car at the North Hollywood Park. "Out," she said. "We're almost there."

Davy looked around, disappointed. "The park? This your hideout?" he asked.

"No, stupid, I said we were *almost* there." She reached into the back seat and grabbed a blanket. "Come one," she said.

The two walked past the clubhouse, where a group of senior citizens were sunning on benches, then past the children's play area. Squeals of kids on swings followed them as they passed the players on the ball field and crossed an expanse of grass. They stopped where a narrow wash, lined with trees and shrubs, cut across the park.

"Now what?" said Davy, looking around.

"Follow me," Maxi said. She started down the steep incline into the wash.

Wonderingly, Davy followed her down to the floor of the wash, a concrete channel crisscrossing the entire city. It was constantly dry except for a rainy few weeks in the winter, when it filled up with swiftly rushing runoff water to the delight of small children, and to the dismay of the Fire Department, who occasionally had to fish the kids out, sometimes at the point of drowning.

Maxi folded the blanket and laid it down against one of the steep cement walls of the wash. She sat down and patted the blanket. "Sit," she said.

Davy sat beside her and leaned back. The park, the people, the streets, everything was blissfully gone. He looked around. It was like a hidden valley, the golden sky filtering through the overhung branches.

Maxi fished into her handbag and brought out a pint of vodka. She took a swig and handed the bottle to Davy. "Refreshments," she said.

Davy took a drink and set the bottle down between them. Reclining against the wall of the wash, they watched the clouds—hurried by the wind—separate, roll, touch, then shape and re-shape.

"There's a castle," said Maxi.

"Looks more like a cloud to me."

"It's a castle," said Maxi firmly.

"A cloud. Cumulus."

"You're blind. It's a castle. With a tower on top."

"Okay," smiled Davy. "It's a castle."

"There's a girl in the tower," said Maxi dreamily. "She's beautiful . . . long, silky hair . . . blue eyes . . ."

"Yeah," said Davy. He thought of Linda.

"She's a princess . . . Princess Maxine . . ."

Davy could see Linda, dressed in a long, flowing gown, arms outstretched, waiting to receive him.

"See the dragon?"

"Where?" said Davy.

"Over there, on the right . . . see it?"

"Stratus," said Davy. "That's a stratus."

"It's a dragon. No, a monster. A slimy monster breathing white smoke."

Davy laughed. It did kind of resemble a monster, looked at in a certain way. "Okay, it's a monster."

". . . breathing white, poisonous smoke," said Maxi. "And if the vapors happen to touch you, you are consumed by them." Maxi deepened her voice and intoned, ". . . poisonous vapors consuming you . . . disintegrating your body into thin air . . ."

And the clouds backdropped her words by twisting into spiraling, vaporous plumes.

Maxi went on: "And the princess is waiting . . . she's waiting for her lover to rescue her . . ."

Davy closed his eyes. He could see himself in Linda's arms. She was caressing him . . . kissing him . . .

They lay motionless for a while. Then:

"Davy?"

"Hmm?"

"Do you think Linda's beautiful?"

"She's okay."

"Know what I wish?" said Maxi.

"What?"

Maxi sat up and laughed. "I wish I had another drink," she said, reaching for the bottle.

In the days and weeks that followed, Davy and Maxi met almost every day after school and went to the wash. Sometimes they talked; Maxi told him about her father—how he worked at a snack bar in the bowling alley, how he had been drinking steadily for two years, ever since her mother died. And Davy found it easy to talk to her. For the first time in his life, he could tell someone how he felt, inside. And she listened, she understood. She was, truly, his pal. Not once did she refer to that drunken night in her camper, and Davy was grateful to her for that.

Sometimes Davy and Maxi felt no need to talk at all; they could simply sit quietly, side by side. Davy had a friend at last; a real friend.

And each day he found himself wishing the time away, waiting for the hours they could be together; he and Maxi and the bottle.

4

It was a Friday afternoon and, as usual, Davy waited for Maxi at the car on Cedros Street. It had been raining most of the day, but now the sun shone and the air smelled clean and fresh. Davy was looking forward to going to the wash with Maxi.

Maxi approached the car. Her eyes were sparkling and her face was flushed. "I have to take you straight home," she announced. "Get in the car, I'll tell you about it."

In the car, they headed toward Davy's house. "I'm having a party tonight. I've so much to do . . . shopping, cleaning the house . . ."

"Hold on," interrupted Davy. "What party? What are you talking about?"

"My father's off fishing with the camper this weekend. I told Mike about it. So we're having a party. At my house. Tonight."

"But we were going to the movies," said Davy.

"We can go to the movies anytime," said Maxi. "Mike invited the crowd; Paul, Cliff, Barbara . . . the whole gang will be there."

"I don't know," said Davy. "I guess I'll skip it." He still felt uncomfortable in the company of the gang.

Maxi's face fell. "But Davy, you've got to come! I need you!" She laughed ruefully. "Tell you the truth, I've never had a party at my house before. I'm a little scared."

Davy looked at her. He'd never seen her so excited. She seemed like a little kid, defenseless, vulnerable. She flashed him a pleading look. "Oh Davy, I'm counting on you!"

He didn't want to go to the party. He didn't want to risk being the butt of the guys' jokes again. He cringed just thinking about it.

Maxi's voice sounded anxious. "Linda said she'd come early," she said, "to help me set up. Please come, Davy."

Linda. He hadn't heard her name said in days now. Of course, Linda would be there. "Okay," he said. "I'll come."

"Oh, Davy, you're a doll! I love you!" Maxi flushed. "I mean, you're a terrific friend."

Maxi pulled the Camaro up to Davy's house. "Don't be late," she smiled at him gratefully.

"I won't," said Davy.

"And don't forget, it's B.Y.O.B., bring your own bottle."

All afternoon Davy worried about how he was to get a bottle of booze. It was easy enough for Maxi. Her father brought home whiskey from the bowling alley bar. He never remembered how much he had so it was simple for her to take whatever she wanted. He never knew the difference. All this time, Maxi had been generously sharing her stock with Davy. But it wasn't so easy for him. Ever since he'd come home drunk, his dad had kept an eye on the liquor supply.

He went into his bedroom and checked the tin money box he kept in his bottom drawer. Nine dollars and change. Plenty. But how was he going to buy the booze? The storekeepers lost their licence if they were caught selling to a minor. Nobody took the chance.

Well, he could try. He sometimes passed for older. What could he lose? Worst that could happen is that he'd be refused.

Davy hung around outside the corner liquor store until the customers had left. Then he went and stood at the counter.

"Well?" said the proprietor. "What can I do for you?"

"Bottle of scotch," said Davy softly.

"What's that?"

"A bottle of scotch," repeated Davy.

The storekeeper appraised him. "Run along

sonny," he said sarcastically. "Come back later—in a few years, punk."

Embarrassed, Davy slunk out of the store. He started for home. Maxi would have enough booze for him. But he didn't like the way that thought made him feel. He turned and walked in the opposite direction. Why should he always be mooching from Maxi? All the kids would be bringing their own bottles. He would, too.

Davy walked to the chain drugstore a couple of blocks away. It was always crowded. The checkers barely had time to look up. Maybe, if he bought some other stuff as well, the checker wouldn't notice his age.

In the store, Davy took a bottle of scotch off the shelf. He looked around. The checkstands were busy, the crowd thick. Why should he take a chance on being embarrassed again? He could simply walk out. Heart pounding, he slipped the bottle under his jacket and made his way out the door. Then he ran all the way home.

Once he was safely in his own room, he sat on the bed and took a drink from the stolen bottle. He stashed the bottle under the bed and lay down. I'm a thief, he thought miserably. Then: Ahh, they'll never miss it—big company like that, they can afford it.

But somehow, he felt dirty; guilty and dirty.

Maxi passed around a bowl of potato chips to the kids sitting and standing around. Davy stood to the side watching Linda. He would have liked to dance with her, hold her in his arms. But nobody was dancing to the wild blasts of rock music, so he sat down at the end of the sofa watching her flirt first with one guy then with another.

Maxi tried real hard to make the party a success. She kept sending kids to the dining room table to try the dips, cheese, crackers, and other goodies. Most of the kids drank. The Cokes and mixes went fast.

Davy noticed after a while that some couples went off into the bedrooms, or to the back patio to smoke a joint. Then somebody started the drinking games. Davy joined in. He had the most fun in the relay race, where each player had to take a drink before running the length of the living room and hand his glass to the next man, who had to take a drink before his turn. At the end of the race, nobody knew who had won, but everybody was high.

By midnight, almost all the guests had gone, but Mike and his gang stayed on. Mike stood up. He drew a pack of playing cards from his pocket. "All right, gang, gather around the kitchen table for a game of chug-a-lug," he said. "Ladies first," he said, ushering Linda, Barbara and Ellen to the table.

Davy didn't know what was up. But he was

soon in the thick of the game. Low man in a five-card poker hand had to drink half a glass of booze, straight. The game dragged on for a while with no one getting drunk enough to fall off his chair or lie down.

"Hey," said Paul during the lull in the game. "Why don't we make the game more interesting? Next low man strips naked, okay?"

"You're on!" said Stan.

"Everyone game?" asked Paul.

"Okay," said Linda. "Everyone's in. My deal." She turned to Maxi. "I need a Coke," she said. "Get me one, will you, Maxi?"

"Sure," said Maxi, rising to go into the dining room.

As soon as Maxi left the room, Linda quickly drew five low cards out of the deck and put them in Maxi's place. Then she dealt to the others. Maxi came back with the Coke for Linda.

Davy knew what he should do. He should stop the game and tell them all the party was over. He should tell Maxi that Linda cheated against her. He should save Maxi from being hurt and embarrassed. But he said nothing.

Ellen, Stan's date, turned her cards up first. She had two fives, a six and a four. She squealed when the boys jibed her about undressing, but her protest wasn't real. They all knew Maxi would show up with the lowest hand.

Davy's turn was next. He had one ten and the rest pictures.

Maxi turned her cards over. She stared down at them as the other kids screamed and hooted.

"Off with her clothes, off with her clothes!" said Mike.

"Take 'em off, take 'em off!" sang Cliff.

Maxi pushed her chair back and stood up. She flicked a desperate look at Davy.

"No," she said. "I'm not playing. Somebody cheated. You all cheated when I left the room."

"Who you calling cheaters?" said Linda. "You lost, you pay the consequences."

Davy looked at Maxi. Her face was scarlet. "Leave her alone," he said.

"Come on, stop stalling. Strip," said Linda coldly.

"I won't," Maxi said.

Cliff rose. "We'll help you," he said, coming around the table. He grabbed her by the shoulders, but she squirmed out of his grasp.

"Get away from me!" said Maxi, panic in her voice.

Suddenly, the kids had her surrounded. "Hold her, hold her!" yelled Cliff.

"Get her on the floor!" shouted Mike.

They forced Maxi down on the floor, then they all got around her and held her down.

"Ouch, she bit me!" wailed Ellen.

"Stop it! Let me go!" Maxi screamed, struggling. But there were too many of them. And they were too determined.

Davy felt he ought to do something, but he didn't have the nerve to take them all on. He watched helplessly while the gang ripped and tore her clothes off. "I've got her blouse!" said Barbara triumphantly.

Laughing, Linda slipped Maxi's panties off her while the others held her down. She forced off her bra and dangled it above her head.

Maxi was stripped.

They all stood in a circle laughing at her while she sat up and placed her hands over her breasts. Tears streaming down her face, she looked up at them wild-eyed and panting.

Despite his reluctance, Davy felt himself breaking through the circle. He pulled his jacket off and threw it over Maxi. "Okay, the party's over," he said. "Go home."

Davy and Maxi were sitting on the floor in front of the fireplace. Maxi had put her robe on and turned down the lights so Davy couldn't see her tear-stained face.

"Want me to help you clean up?" asked Davy.

"I'll do it tomorrow," said Maxi. "They shouldn't have done it," she added softly.

"No," said Davy.

"They wouldn't do a thing like that to Linda."

Davy didn't answer. She was right.

"They think I'm cheap; they hate me."

"They don't hate you. That's their idea of fun."

"Linda was the worst of them," said Maxi. "And I thought she was my friend."

They sat quietly and stared into the fire.

"Davy?"

"Hmm?"

"You like her, don't you?"

"She's okay," Davy hedged.

"I don't blame you. She's beautiful."

Davy looked at Maxi. With the soft firelight flickering over her she looked delicate and pretty. She looked lovely. "There's nothing wrong with you."

"You're just saying that," said Maxi. "All the guys are crazy about Linda."

"I'm not. Not anymore. I'm crazy about *you*," said Davy, surprised at his own words.

She turned and looked into his eyes. "Honest?"

"I like you better than any girl I know," said Davy.

"Even Linda?"

"Even Linda."

Maxi lay down with her head in Davy's lap. For a long time there was silence except for the crackling of the fire. Then:

"Know what I see?" Maxi said.

"Where?"

"In the fire. I can see pictures, can't you?"

"Like the clouds?"

"Yeah, like that."

"You're a weirdo, but I like you anyway," laughed Davy.

"No, really. I see two people. You and me. We're holding hands."

Davy took her hand. He helped her into a sitting position and cupped her chin in his hand. Then he kissed her gently on the mouth.

Maxi undid the cord on her robe and let it slip off her shoulders. He felt a catch in his throat as the red glow of the fire played over her body.

A tingling sense of urgency filled him as she lay back down on the floor, pulling him along with her.

5

As spring deepened and the weather grew warmer, Davy and Maxi were inseparable. They took little trips to Disneyland and other places; they spent long, quiet hours talking at the wash; they went to drive-in movies, skating rinks; they hiked on the beach; they made love in the camper. And everywhere they went, they took their third partner—the bottle.

Davy was happy. He was no longer alone. He had his girl, and he felt at home in the world. And he no longer had to feel guilty or sneaky about his drinking. He could drink openly with Maxi; she drank the way he did.

He had bouts with diarrhea. He was spending more and more time retching on his knees in front of the toilet. But so did Maxi; they laughed about it. They tried dozens of hangover remedies. They tried sticking to one kind of booze; they tried drinking and eating together; but they still suffered hangovers. And if they forgot to eat regularly, they never forgot to drink.

Davy began to lie about his loss of appetite to his mother. He told her he had to keep trim because he wanted to go out for track at school. Other times he'd say he'd eaten at a friend's house, or that he'd had a big lunch. But his loss of appetite continued. He just wasn't eating. He didn't care, but finally, to get her off his back, he forced himself to eat in her presence until she began to relax.

It was Saturday evening. Davy's mother and dad had gone out for dinner and he was alone in the house. He was getting ready to go out with Maxi. Tonight, they were going to fool around downtown at Olvera Street, maybe go to Chinatown afterward.

The telephone rang. It was Maxi. "Davy, listen, it's terrible! I don't know what to do!"

"What's wrong?"

"My father . . ."

"What happened?"

"He caught me in the camper . . . drinking . . . he had a fit . . ."

"He hit you?"

"Worse, he took all the booze and left the house."

"So?"

"So, there's not a drop around. What'll we do for tonight?"

52

"You've got that fake I.D. We'll use it. I've got money."

"I tried that this afternoon. It didn't work. They wouldn't sell me any."

"Don't worry," Davy said. "I'll think of something."

"Well, hurry over," said Maxi. "I need a drink."

Davy hung up. They could try using the fake I.D. someplace downtown. But what if it didn't work there, either?

He went into the bathroom to check his cough syrup bottle. He'd filled it up at Maxi's house just the other day. The bottle was half full. Hell, that wouldn't last them an hour. He put the bottle back.

Davy thought about his father's bottles in the den. There was nothing else he could do. He went into the den and looked around. He was in luck. He found an empty bottle in the wastebasket. He poured some liquor into it, added water to the first one, and put it back on the shelf. The color was only slightly lighter. His father would never know.

Maxi was sitting in the Camaro when Davy arrived. She reached over and opened the door for him. "Did you get any? God, I'm dying for a drink," she said.

He handed her the bottle.

She took a drink, then looked at the bottle. "That's not very much," she said mournfully.

"Start driving," said Davy. "Maybe we can get some old guy downtown to buy us some."

Maxi crossed her fingers. "Leave us pray," she said.

By the time they got off the freeway, they had emptied the bottle. But Davy was feeling confident. He spotted a run-down liquor store. "Stop here," he said.

Maxi parked the car at the curb. "What now?" she asked.

A middle-aged man in working clothes was coming up the street. "Let's see if we can get that man to buy for us," said Davy.

They got out of the car and waited until the man reached them. "Let me do the talking," said Davy.

"We'll give you a couple of bucks if you buy us some booze," he said to the man.

"Beat it, little boy," said the man, pushing him aside.

"Guess we're out of luck," said Maxi as the man walked away.

"Not yet," said Davy. He nodded at three tough-looking guys coming down the street. They looked to be in their twenties.

"This time, let me," Maxi said.

"Right," said Davy. "They won't refuse a girl." He handed her a ten-dollar bill.

Maxi approached the guy in the middle. He

was a big man with a black mustache and long, wet-looking hair pulled back in a ponytail. She waved the bill in front of him. "Buy us some whiskey, mister?" she said.

The fellow looked her up and down until Davy came and put his hand on her arm. "This your boy friend?"

Maxi nodded. "Buy us some booze?"

"Should we buy them some booze?" sneered one, a redhead. "What do you say, guys, want to do the little girl a favor?"

"I don't know," said the first one. "Buying booze for kids; we could get in big trouble."

"Come on," said Maxi. "We'll pay you for your trouble."

"Why not?" said the third guy. "We're Boy Scouts, ain't we? Ain't we Boy Scouts?"

"Okay," said the first guy. "What kind you want?"

"Scotch," said Maxi. "The cheapest they've got." She handed him the money and the three went into the liquor store.

Maxi grinned. "That was easy. Didn't know I had so much sex appeal."

"I didn't like the way they looked at you," said Davy uneasily.

"Who cares how they looked at me, we get our booze, don't we?"

The three toughs came out of the store and, without looking at them, walked breezily by.

"Hey, where you going?" said Maxi.

"Get lost," the mustached man said menacingly.

"Come on," said Davy. "Give us our bottle and our change."

"What bottle? What change?" said the redhead. He turned to his friends. "You know anything about any bottles, any change?"

"Naw," said one. "Never heard anything about it."

The redhead laughed. "Go home to your mommy, kiddies."

Maxi reached for the paper bag. "Give us our booze," she said.

The man caught her arm with his free hand and twisted it. "You don't want to get hurt, do you, baby?" he sneered.

"Ouch, let go of me!" Maxi cried.

"Take your hands off her!" said Davy.

The man dropped Maxi's arm and pushed her away. He stepped over to Davy, his pals close behind him. "Who you giving orders?" he said. He touched Davy's cheek with a finger and leered at him. "Stand aside, move it."

Davy stood his ground, the muscles in his cheek twitching.

"Never mind, let's go, Davy," said Maxi nervously.

Davy tried to be cool but he felt a gathering of outrage in his chest. "I'll take our bottle and our money first," he said, clenching his fists.

"Up yours," said the mustached man. He and his friends walked on for a few steps.

"Bastards!" Davy said to their backs.

They turned back to Davy. "What did you say?" the redhead said slowly.

"I said you're bastards!" Full of rage now, Davy didn't care what he said. "You rotten sons of bitches!"

And that's when they struck. As if one of them had given an order, the three pounced at once. It all happened so swiftly that Davy had no time to steel himself for a fight, or even protect himself with his arms.

They jumped all over him, all three together, hitting him high and low, throwing him to the ground, where his head hit the cement. Fists punched at him, fingernails tore at his face.

He felt a sudden blazing pain in his groin; someone was kicking him. Over the savage buzzing in his head, he heard Maxi screaming: "Davy! Davy! Help! Somebody help!"

A hot, rasping voice said, "Smack her! Shut her up!"

Maxi cried out in pain.

The punches fell upon Davy with no letup, on his head, his chest, his back. Another violent kick smashed at his abdomen, and he felt the wind escape from his stomach. He gasped, fighting for air. At last, his breath came back with a rush, and he felt himself lose control as urine gushed down into his pants. He clutched his arms around his body and curled up to hide himself.

He could hear mumbling above him, then a kick in the lower back like a bolting, piercing flame.

He heard the deep voice of another man. Was it the liquor store owner? "Stop! Bums! Hoodlums! Get out of here!"

Now the sound of running feet receding, and then he melted into a syrupy haze.

It was dark; safe and black and quiet. Then somebody was prodding him and he groped upward from his brief blackout. His head was cradled in Maxi's arms. The liquor store proprietor loomed above them. "Do you want me to call the police, the ambulance?" he asked.

"No," said Maxi. "Please, just help me to the car."

In a murky fog, Davy rose unsteadily to his knees, his body racked with pain, while the man and Maxi put him into the car. Davy felt as if his body was torn apart, his legs rubbery, showers of pain stabbing at him.

As Maxi started the car, he heard a strange, sobbing sound. Then he realized the sound was coming from himself. Head lolling, he was whimpering like an injured puppy.

"I'll take you to a hospital. You're hurt bad," said Maxi.

"No . . . no hospital . . . the camper . . ."

He squinted at her from his already puffing

eyes. Her forehead was bruised and she had red finger marks on her arm. He let his head fall onto the back of the seat and he closed his eyes.

Every jolt of the car made him cry out in pain; cut his breath. The ride seemed endless, but they finally made it home.

In the camper at last, Maxi bathed his face, the cold water inflaming the fresh cuts and bruises. She brought him a clean pair of her father's pants, then made him lie down on the bunk. He lay perfectly still, afraid to relax, not stirring, feeling a dull ache down to his marrow.

Maxi lay down beside him and took his hand. And then he slept.

"Davy . . . Davy . . . it's eleven o'clock."

Davy was instantly awake. Painfully, he rose on one elbow. It seemed as though his very bones were on fire. He lay back on the pillow and groaned.

"You'll have to go soon," Maxi said.

"Not yet," said Davy.

Maxi lit a cigarette. "I've been thinking," she said. She waited a moment. "Are you listening?"

"I'm listening." He felt thirsty. He tried to wet his lips. "I need a drink," he said.

"That's what I want to talk to you about," said Maxi. "About our drinking."

"Everybody drinks," said Davy.

"Not like us . . . not like we do. We've got to clean up our act. Get it together."

She was right. He knew it. He had known it for a long time. His grades at school were at the danger point, he was losing weight, and when he wasn't drinking, he was thinking about it. Even tonight . . . what happened tonight was because of the drinking. Tonight, they could have been killed . . . both of them.

"Davy, you mad?"

"I'm not mad."

"Let's make a promise . . . a pledge to each other. No more drinking, okay?" Maxi said.

Davy thought about it. He knew he could quit anytime he wanted to. He just never wanted to. But it might be different for Maxi. She'd been drinking longer than he, and she drank more . . . lots more. He had to quit for her sake.

"Once my dad went to Alcoholics Anonymous," Maxi said. "They help people there. Maybe we should check it out."

"What for?" said Davy. "We just quit, didn't we?"

Maxi turned over and kissed him on the cheek. "I love you," she said softly.

"I love you, too," said Davy.

6

Davy was in luck. His folks were asleep by the time he got home.

The next morning, he awakened bitter-mouthed, the sounds of breakfast in the kitchen reaching him. A flash of anxiety came over him as he thought of having to face them.

Davy took a warm bath and put on a turtle-neck T-shirt. He taped the cuts on his forehead and cheek, but there was no way he could hide all the damage. His face was swollen and dis-colored, his eyes practically closed. He'd have to tell them something. He could tell them he'd been jumped by some muggers. No, they'd want to call the police. He could tell them there had been a car accident. But they'd ask too many questions. He might get Maxi in trou-ble.

He wondered if he should tell the truth. They wouldn't like it, but at least he could say he wasn't going to drink anymore. It would be a relief to get everything out in the open, at last; not to have to lie anymore.

He put the adhesive tape back into the medicine chest and automatically reached for his cough syrup bottle. He could use a drink. He let his hand drop to his side. He must be flipping out. Didn't he just decide to come clean with his parents? And that pledge he'd made to Maxi. He wouldn't go back on it.

Davy went into the kitchen. His mother gave a little cry when she looked at him. "Oh my God . . . Davy . . . what happened?"

"What the hell!" said Frank, dropping his newspaper.

"I'm all right," said Davy weakly. He sat down stiffly at the table and faced his parents.

"Oh, Davy, Davy . . ." wailed his mother.

"Good Lord, what happened to you?" said Frank.

"There was a fight," Davy blurted out before he could change his mind about telling the truth. "Some guys jumped me . . ."

"Jumped you!" said Frank. "We'll take you to the hospital! The police . . . we'll call the police . . ."

"No," said Davy. "Listen, I was drinking . . ."

"Drinking!" blasted his father. "I thought I told you to stay away from the stuff . . . I told you . . ."

"Frank, he's hurt. Please, Frank . . ." his mother started.

"Drinking!" his father yelled. "Like some skid-row bum! You're nothing but a dumb punk ... a dumb, punk kid!"

"Frank, stop it ... the boy's hurt!"

"Good! I'm glad! Maybe this'll teach him! Get something through his thick skull; he doesn't listen to anything *I* say!"

"What do you ever say to him?" said Martha angrily. "You never give him two minutes of your precious time!"

"I'm on the road! Trying to make a living! What am I supposed to do? Stay home and be his keeper?"

"You can be a father to him when you *are* home! You never pay him any attention ... you ignore us both! When's the last time you really talked to him ... talked to me?"

Bewildered, Davy looked from one parent to the other. They were glaring at each other with raw hatred in their eyes, and he suddenly realized they had *never* liked each other.

"It's your fault!" yelled Frank. "Why don't you look after him? I can't be in two places at once. The kid becomes a drunk right in front of your eyes and you've got your head in some book!"

His mother began to cry. "I have to do something—I'm alone—I'm bored ..."

"If you were doing your job, you wouldn't have time to be bored! What do you want? You want me to stay home . . . baby-sit . . . entertain you?"

"Hey, wait a minute," said Davy. "It's nobody's fault but mine."

His parents ignored him. It was as though he wasn't even in the room.

"You're out there having a good time, doing what you want, going where you want!" shouted Martha. "You only come home for a change of clothes! You're not interested in your son or me! You may as well not be married at all!"

"I've given that some thought, believe me!" said his father. "I work hard all week . . . come home to a whining wife . . . a drunken son! You've got everything you need . . . a nice house, clothes . . ." He turned to Davy. "Is there anything you need? Everything's handed to you, maybe that's the trouble! What are you doing to yourself? What are you doing to us?"

"I'm trying to tell you," said Davy helplessly.

"Why don't you listen to him? For once, listen to him!" said Martha.

"All right," said Frank. He sat back in his chair. "I'm listening. Go on, talk!" he said to Davy.

"I'm trying to tell you . . . what happened," said Davy. "I didn't mean it to be like this."

"Like what?" said Frank. "Like what? Go on, tell me, I'm listening," he challenged.

"Like this," said Davy. "I didn't mean to get hooked on it."

"Hooked!" Martha turned pale. "What do you mean, 'hooked'?"

"I don't know. It's like the more I drink, the more I need to." He shot his father a pleading look. "But it's all right. I'm off it now, I promise. I was thinking, maybe I'd go to Alcoholics Anonymous."

"You're not an alcoholic!" said Martha, horrified.

"No son of mine is going to associate with a bunch of drunks!" roared Frank. "Not on your life!"

"We can get him some counseling . . . a psychiatrist. Frank, he needs help, can't you see that?"

"What he needs is a good kick in the ass!" Frank shot back.

"See what I mean?" said Martha. "Why can't we talk . . . like a family?"

"Okay, we're talking," said Frank. "That what you think you need, a psychiatrist?" he said to Davy sarcastically.

Davy looked at his father mutely. His body ached and he was beginning to feel shaky. What he needed was a drink.

"Answer me! Why don't you answer me!" said his father.

Martha got up and put her hand on Davy's shoulder. "You're like an animal!" she said to Frank. "How can he answer you when you're badgering him like that?"

Enraged, Frank rose, knocking over his chair. "Do what you want with him! Take him to some shrink, whatever! I can't fight the both of you!" he said, storming out of the room.

Davy hung around in his room for a while after breakfast. He wondered how Maxi was. But he couldn't keep his mind on her. His attention was on the rise and fall of angry voices from the living room. He had to get out of there, out of the house. He'd get on his bike and ride someplace. Maybe he could work some of the soreness out of his muscles.

Without thinking of where he was going, Davy found himself on Magnolia Boulevard riding toward the park. The warm sun on his back felt soothing, and his muscles were beginning to loosen up.

When he got to the park, he took a long drink from the water fountain then found a bench in the shadow of a huge Chinese elm and parked his bike. The branches made a kind of cave over one end of the bench, and for a moment he felt comforted, protected.

From the open windows of the clubhouse behind him came gusts of music, where the senior citizens were having a meeting. A kid, about eleven or twelve years old, whizzed by on a skateboard. Davy sighed. The kid looked pretty good keeping his balance on that thing. Davy's eyes followed him until he rounded a bend in the path and glided out of sight.

An old, beat-up bum came down the path, leaned against a trash can, and began drinking from a bottle in a paper bag. Davy's throat felt so dry he could hardly swallow as he watched the man drink. He wet his parched lips, almost tasting the booze going down warm and easy. He began to sweat and his hands were shaking. He wanted a drink—he flat-out *had* to have a drink!

He forgot his pledge, his promise, everything, as he walked over to the old man. "How about a drink?" he said, trying to act cool.

The man stiffened and clutched his bag to his skinny chest. He looked at Davy. "Run off and play, sonny," he said. His stinking breath almost knocked Davy out, but he kept his eyes on the bag.

"Come on, give a guy a break," said Davy, reaching out for the bag.

The man stepped backward and gaped a wide, toothless smile. "Go ask your mama for the tit, little boy." he cackled. Then he turned and stumbled down the path. There was a dark, wet stain on the back of his baggy pants.

Stung, Davy felt his face flush. He stood there clenching and unclenching his fists. Hot tears fell on his cheeks and he brushed them angrily away with the back of his hand.

He got on his bike and pumped vigorously all the way home.

Davy's parents sat in icy silence all through dinner. His mother's eyes were puffed from crying and his father never looked in his direction.

Davy kept glancing at the clock. It had been almost twenty-four hours since he had a drink and his nerves were raw and tingling. He had the weirdest sensation of wanting to yell . . . to scream at the top of his lungs. His hands were shaking so, he needed to use both of them to raise his glass to his lips.

He wondered how Maxi was doing. He'd called her as soon as he got home, but the line had been busy. As soon as he could get away from the table, he'd call again.

His father put his coffee cup down. "I have to see Wilson in Bakersfield first thing in the morning." he said. "I'll be leaving in an hour."

Martha flicked him a look, opened her mouth to say something, then simply nodded.

A feeling of guilt engulfed Davy. His parents had quarreled over him. Suppose his father went away and never came back again? Suppose they decided to get divorced? He would be responsible.

Davy pushed his dessert away and got up. "I'm sorry," he said. Then he ran into his room.

While Martha was doing the dishes Davy heard his father slam the door on his way out of the house.

Martha poked her head into Davy's room. "I'll be in my room . . . studying," she said. But when she closed her door, Davy could hear the sound of muffled crying.

He crept out of his room and went to the kitchen telephone.

"Hello, Maxi?"

"Yes," said a weak voice.

"How you doing?"

"Not so good," said Maxi.

"You haven't been drinking?"

There was a short laugh. "Are you kidding? Oh, Davy it's awful. I feel like I'm splitting apart."

"I don't feel so hot myself," said Davy.

"Davy?"

"Yeah?"

"I'm scared."

"Scared?"

"I fell asleep this afternoon . . . or maybe I wasn't asleep, I don't know . . ."

"Yeah?"

"I saw things . . . bugs . . . giant ones . . . crawling all over . . . all over the room . . . all over me."

"You were dreaming," said Davy.

"My hands are shaking so bad I have to sit

69

on them to keep them still. And I have these cold sweats."

"Maybe you should have a drink," said Davy. "Just one to get you over this. Maybe you shouldn't quit so suddenly."

"No, we made a pledge, a bargain. I'll stick it out."

"Go to bed," said Davy. "Maybe you can sleep it off."

"I'm afraid," Maxi said. "I'm afraid if I sleep . . . those dreams . . . they may come back. Oh, Davy, I'm afraid to sleep and afraid not to."

"Want me to come over?"

"No, don't come. I look awful. I don't want you to see me like this."

"Will you be okay?"

"I'll be okay. Just tell me once more."

"Tell you what?"

"You know."

Davy chuckled. "I love you," he whispered.

"I love you," she said.

When Davy awakened the next morning it was after ten. He stumbled into the kitchen for a cup of coffee. His mother was at the stove. "I didn't wake you," she said. "You couldn't go to school looking like this anyway.

"No," said Davy. "I guess not."

"Sit down," said Martha, handing him a mug of coffee.

The two sat down at the table. "I've been

calling all morning," said Martha. "We have an appointment with a psychiatrist this afternoon."

"Today?" said Davy. He really didn't think she'd go through with the psychiatrist bit. He thought she'd forget about it, let it pass.

His mother nodded. "We were lucky. This man comes highly recommended. We have to be there at four." She looked at him. "Don't be so worried. The doctor knows how to handle these things."

Davy felt a cold ball of fear at the pit of his stomach, an overpowering, unreasoning fear. What was he afraid of? The doctor? What could the doctor do to him? But the doctor could find out, he could expose him. Find out what? Expose what? Davy was confused. Beads of perspiration formed on his forehead.

"Listen, Davy, you're sick, you need help. It'll be all right, believe me." She smiled. "Why don't you go back to bed? I'll bring your breakfast in to you."

The way he felt right now, he'd go anywhere, do anything. Maybe the psychiatrist could really do something to help him.

Davy let his mother wait on him. It seemed to make her feel better. Besides, he had no strength to protest. He felt washed out, limp. His body was crying for a drink, raging for it. He tried to shake the feeling. He ate his breakfast, dozed, took a shower, prowled around his room, tried to read. But nothing could diminish

71

the craving, the phantom smell and taste of a drink, the fantasy of going into the bathroom and polishing off what was left in the cough syrup bottle.

All day, Davy suffered an unquenchable thirst. He drank ice water, juice, coffee; the thirst persisted. He was racked with violent cramps and spurts of diarrhea. In turn, his skin felt damp, crawly, itchy; his scalp felt prickly.

At last it was time to leave the house. A streak of pain clutched at his gut and he ran into the bathroom. Another episode of diarrhea, and then Davy hung weakly over the sink splashing water over his face.

"Coming?" he heard his mother call.

"I'm coming," he said.

He straightened, trying to pull himself together. He started out of the room, turned, opened the medicine chest, and took out the cough syrup bottle. He couldn't help it. He had to have that drink! He had to have that drink! He gulped down what was left in the bottle and eyes watering, let it warm him.

"We'll be late," called Martha.

Quickly, he brushed his teeth, then walked out of the bathroom feeling better already. His mood lifted, brightened; he was flooded with a sense of well-being.

Martha sat in the waiting room while Davy was being interviewed by the doctor.

"You're an intelligent young man," said Dr. Klein. "I won't try to kid you. If you're an alcoholic, you have a killer disease—nothing to be ashamed of—a disease. But you're the one to decide if you want to do something about it."

Davy looked at the doctor. He was a youngish man with a prematurely bald head. What did that smart-ass know about it? He probably never got drunk in his life.

The doctor went on: "Alcoholism is an addiction, the same as with any other drug. It gives you a false high, you become dependent on it."

Shit, thought Davy. I'm not exactly shooting heroin or anything. What's the big deal?

"You have to ask yourself some questions, Davy. Have you withdrawn from your social life, your family? Are you constantly drinking more? Do you have two or three drinks where one used to do? Do you need it to get through tough situations? Are you hiding bottles, getting into trouble over drinking?" He paused. "You don't have to answer me, you have to answer yourself."

Davy looked at the doctor coldly. He sounded as though he was reading from a textbook.

"You have to make up your mind to want to help yourself," said the doctor.

If I have to do everything myself, what's he getting paid for? Davy thought.

"What are you thinking, Davy?" said the doctor.

"I drink too much. I know that, but I'm not an alcoholic."

Davy envisioned the picture of a skid-row bum, a wino. He wasn't like them. "I can lick it myself," he said.

"Whatever you say," said Dr. Klein. "Just remember, if you ever want to get to the source of the trouble, I'm here to help."

"Sure," said Davy. "Thanks."

"The only condition is that I won't treat a wet drunk. It's a waste of time—his and mine. If you want me to help you, you'll have to quit drinking altogether."

Hell, if I quit drinking, why would I need you? thought Davy bitterly.

The man rose and came around the desk. He smiled and shook Davy's hand. "Let me know what you decide after you think about it for a while."

Davy stood up. "I will," he said.

Disappointed and despondent, Davy left the office. The visit had been a bust.

7

"Well, what do you think?" said Martha, heading the car home. "Do you think the doctor can help you?"

"I don't need him," said Davy.

"What do you mean? What did he say to you?"

"He asked about my childhood, all that stuff," said Davy.

Martha sighed. "We could have done better by you," she said guiltily.

"You did fine," said Davy. "Forget it."

"Davy, if you're thinking of the money . . ."

"It's not that. He won't treat me unless I quit drinking. I already quit drinking. I don't need a doctor."

"Maybe this wasn't the right man . . . we could go to another . . ."

"No. No more doctors," Davy interrupted.

Martha looked at him and said nothing more.

His mother stopped the car in front of the

house. "I don't have to go to school. I can stay home with you," she said.

"I'm fine," said Davy. "I'll probably take in a movie or something. Go to your class. You'll be late."

In the house, Davy ate some soup and a dish of pudding. He went to the phone to call Maxi. The phone was answered on the first ring.

"Davy . . . Davy, is that you?"

"You're crying . . . Maxi, what's wrong?"

"I don't know. I feel so weird."

"What do you mean?" He heard muffled sobs. "Maxi, answer me!"

"It's . . . it's hard to explain . . . strange . . . I feel out of it . . . I'm afraid." She spoke between sobs. "Help me, Davy . . . I'm so scared . . . come over please . . . come . . ."

"I'll be right there," said Davy.

Davy let the bike fall on the front lawn of Maxi's house. The house was dark, but there were lights on in the camper.

Maxi was sitting stiffly at the table in the tiny nook. She looked at him. "I came in here. I was afraid to be in the house by myself."

"What's the matter?"

She shrugged. "It's like my head was detached from my body . . . it's like I was a zombie or something."

"I know," said Davy, sliding into the seat opposite her. "It's coming off the stuff that's doing it."

"I suppose so," said Maxi. "I've been figuring it. It's been forty-nine hours since we've had a drink. Oh God, I don't know if I can make it ... I feel so ..."

Suddenly, Maxi stood up. Her body went rigid as though she was electrified. She gave a long, inhuman cry.

"Maxi ... Maxi ... what's the matter?"

Standing board-stiff, her eyes fixed straight ahead, Maxi wailed. "Oooeee . . . oooeee ...oooeee!"

She fell to the floor and her back arched. Eyes rolled back, she began to twitch and shudder, then her arms and legs flailed uncontrollably.

Davy ran to her. Her teeth were clamped tight and she was drooling thick saliva.

Convulsions! thought Davy. My God, she's having convulsions! He tried to remember what he'd learned in first aid about convulsions. The tongue . . . she could choke on her tongue. Her face took on a bluish cast as she thrashed around jerkily.

Davy pinched the sides of her mouth to open it, and pulled her tongue down. He needed something to put between her teeth. With one hand he felt around the tabletop. A spoon. That would be too hard. He reached a paper napkin; then holding the spoon against his stomach, he rolled the napkin around it and put it between her teeth.

Her pelvis was beating upward as Maxi went into violent contortions, flopping heavily. Her head rocked back and forth, her arms pounding the floor.

Davy grabbed pillows from the bunk and shielded her body. He knew he couldn't restrain her. He'd have to let the convulsions have their way; all he could do was keep her from hurting herself. Watching her, he felt a cold, menacing fear grip him.

Slowly, the spasms lessened. Then she relaxed and lay limply inert. Her face was flushed. Her T-shirt was wet with stains, her forehead covered with drops of perspiration.

She opened her eyes and looked at him dully.

"You're all right," said Davy. "Just lie still."

Tears rolled slowly down her face. "What happened?" she said weakly.

"A convulsion," said Davy. "You're all right now." He took her in his arms and held her to his chest. Sitting on the floor, rocking her back and forth, he could feel the tears streaming down his face, mixing with hers.

He carried her to the bunk and laid her down. Now, she began to shiver, her teeth chattering loudly. "I'm cold," she said. "I'm so cold."

Davy covered her with the blanket, put a pillow under her head. He wiped her forehead with his handkerchief. He turned to get another blanket from the closet, but Maxi clutched his hand.

"Don't leave me. Please . . . don't go."

Davy sat on the edge of the bunk and leaned down to kiss her cheek. "I'm here. I'm not going anywhere. I'm staying with you."

He didn't know how long he sat there holding her hand. After a time, her grip relaxed and her breathing became deeply regular. She was asleep.

Now he had time to think. The convulsions were due to the withdrawal from booze, he knew that much. And he knew that whatever happened, he couldn't let her go through anything like that again. If she had cheated with the drinking—broken their pledge as he had—this never would have occurred. She had been true to her word, true to him. He had to do something for her. But what?

He thought of what she had said about Alcoholics Anonymous. They help people with a booze problem. She had sounded willing to go. Okay, then that's where she'd go. He'd go, too—for her sake.

The next day Davy made the call.

"Alcoholics Anonymous, can I help you?" said a cheerful voice on the other end of the phone.

"How old do you have to be . . . I mean, what do you have to do to join?" said Davy.

"All you need is the desire to stop drinking," said the woman's pleasant voice. "Would you like someone to call on you, take you to a meeting?"

"We can get there, my girl friend and I, if you just tell us where and when."

"No problem," said the woman. "We have meetings all over town, day or evening, every day. Where are you?"

When Davy told her, she gave him the name and address of a young people's meeting in Van Nuys for the next night.

Davy and Maxi stopped for a hamburger before the meeting. They sat at an outdoor table and ate quietly, each thinking his own thoughts.

"You nervous?" asked Maxi.

"Naw," Davy said. He was more nervous than he'd want her to know, but he had to be cool for her. What would they find at the meeting? Would they be required to sign anything? Would they meet a bunch of holy rollers, hymn-singers?

"I am," said Maxi. "What if we see someone we know?"

Davy laughed. "Then they'd be there for the same reason we are. What's to worry?"

"That's right," said Maxi giggling. "I never

thought about that." She looked at her watch. "I guess it's time."

"Yeah," said Davy, reluctant to move.

"Do you think they'll help us?" said Maxi.

"Sure they will," Davy said.

Maxi pulled the Camaro up in front of a small one-story stucco building. A sign on the door read: "Van Nuys Club."

"This is it," said Davy.

A boy about eighteen or nineteen greeted them at the door. "Hi," he smiled. "My name is Jim." He shook Davy's hand.

"I'm Davy, this is Maxi," said Davy.

"Haven't seen you around," said Jim. "You new?"

"Yeah," Davy said. "Brand-new."

"Welcome," said Jim. "If you've got a drinking problem, you're in the right place. Go in, look around. There's coffee and doughnuts inside. I'll be along soon."

They passed a room on their right where some kids were playing billiards. Then they came to a large, comfortable lounge-type room, where some girls and boys were manning a snack bar at one end. Kids sat around on colorful sofas and chairs laughing and talking. The two stood and looked around. This could be any clubhouse anywhere.

An attractive girl with long, shining black hair approached them. "My name is Tina," she said. "Jim said to be on the lookout for two newcomers."

"You don't *look* like an alcoholic," Maxi blurted out. She clapped her hand over her mouth. "I mean . . . you look . . . well, you're so . . ."

Tina laughed. She waved her hand around the room. "We're *all* alcoholics, we're just not drunk, that's all. Come on, let's get some coffee." She guided them to the snack bar. "Hey, Rochelle, how about two coffees for two newcomers," she said to the girl behind the counter.

"This your first meeting?" said Rochelle, handing them mugs of coffee. They nodded. "Terrific! Welcome aboard!" she said enthusiastically. "Boy, I can remember my first meeting. I was plenty scared."

"You were plenty messy, too," laughed Tina. "You threw up on the floor in back of the room."

Rochelle laughed uproariously. "Yeah, I was some sloppy drunk! Every time I ever think of taking a drink, I remember that night and change my mind."

They seem to be proud of being alcoholic, proud of being drunks, Davy wondered.

Jim joined them at the snack bar. "I see you've met Tina," he said. "She's an old-timer. Going to take her third birthday cake next week."

"It's your birthday?" said Maxi.

"My AA birthday. After every three hundred sixty-five days of sobriety we get a birthday cake."

Birthday cakes, thought Davy. What a bunch of two-year-olds.

"It sounded crazy to me at first," said Tina. "But those cakes begin to mean more and more each year. You'll see when you get your first one."

"Come on, time for the meeting," said Jim.

They went into a large meeting room with a small raised platform in front. A huge sign behind the podium read: WE CARE; under it was a picture of two clasped hands. Framed readings lined the walls. They were numbered from one to twelve and the first one read: "We admitted we were powerless over alcohol—that our lives had become unmanageable."

Davy and Maxi took seats in back of the room, Tina and Jim on either side of them.

A boy about Davy's age stood at the podium. He rapped the gavel for silence. "Hi, my name is Larry, and I'm an alcoholic," he said.

"Hi Larry!" the group shouted out.

"Are there any other alcoholics here?" he said.

Hands were raised accompanied by whistling, hooting, and laughing.

"Okay, okay, knock it off," Larry laughed. Then he said, "Not to embarrass you or anything, but just to get to know you, are there any newcomers?"

One or two hands were raised in the front rows. Maxi and Davy exchanged looks. Tentatively, Maxi put her hand up. Davy kept his in his lap.

"We'd like to tell the new people that anything they hear tonight may or may not apply to them. Leave anything here that you don't like, take home anything you can use. Now, Lisa will read the twelve steps."

A girl about fourteen came up and read the twelve steps of the Alcoholics Anonymous program. Davy was surprised. The steps hardly mentioned alcohol at all. They seemed like some kind of code of behavior or action.

Another boy read something called the twelve traditions—principles for the group as opposed to the individual. How can these simple rules keep a guy from drinking? Davy thought. They must all be a bunch of morons. He looked around the room. They couldn't *all* be stupid. They looked confident, comfortable. There was something about them that was different . . . what was it?

"Our speaker for tonight is Nathalie F.," said Larry. There was a burst of applause as a girl Davy had seen around school came onto the platform. He remembered her as one of the cheerleaders.

"My name is Nathalie, and I'm an alcoholic," the girl said.

"Hi, Nathalie," chorused the group.

"We're supposed to tell what it used to be like, what happened, and what it's like now." She paused. "I'm kind of nervous, this is my first pitch."

Here it comes, thought Davy disgustedly. The evangelists, the preachers.

The audience applauded and Nathalie smiled and went on: "I had my first drink when I was still in junior high," she said. "It seemed like from that day on, I needed it . . . especially when I had to speak in front of groups . . . like now."

The spectators laughed and there was a smattering of more applause.

Nathalie continued: "I used booze for everything . . . to keep me from being lonely; to cheer me when the other kids teased me about my braces; to give me courage to talk to guys; to keep me from being scared . . ." She stopped talking for a moment and took a drink of water. "I've always been scared, for as long as I can remember. I don't know why, it was like I couldn't measure up or something. I always seemed to be on the outside looking in. Booze gave me the feeling of being someone, belonging. Liquor was my friend, the answer to all my problems."

Maxi took Davy's hand and squeezed it.

"But then my friend turned on me," said Nathalie. "I had hangovers, blackouts . . . I once took a final exam in a blackout; couldn't remember a thing about it." She laughed. "Can you guess the grade I got?

"I began to steal booze; I got into trouble, I crashed my parents' car, was thrown into jail for drunk driving. You'd think that experience would stop me. But it only made me bitter and sorry for myself. It just gave me another excuse to drink.

"And drinking came first in my life. My parents, my friends, school, everything and everyone began to interfere with my drinking. So I did the only thing a sensible girl would do ... I ran away."

There was a murmur of laughter from the crowd and Nathalie laughed, too.

Davy squirmed in his seat. He could see nothing funny in her story. What were all these idiots laughing about?

Nathalie echoed his thoughts. "It may sound funny now," she said. "But it wasn't fun and games then. All alone, I hitchhiked from Los Angeles to San Francisco. For a whole month I was in a drunken fog. I found a group of kids up there who really knew how to live. We spent all our time strung out, boozing it up, popping pills, and smoking pot; we slept where we could, ate when we begged money or food, stole anything else we needed.

"And if you think that was fun," she said, "here's what happened next: we were attacked by a street gang and beaten until we were a pulpy, bloody mess. I can't even remember how the fight started."

Davy stiffened. He heard Maxi draw in her breath.

"I came home and my parents tried to help me, but I wasn't about to be helped. I hated myself, what I was becoming. By now, I had drunk myself out of friends, ambition; my life was a drag. I couldn't hack it anymore. All I wanted to do was die, kill myself. And even at that, I was a failure. I took an overdose, but all that happened was that I slept for two days."

Davy heard Maxi sniffling. He looked at her. She was dabbing her eyes with her handkerchief.

"When I came to, I'd had it," said Nathalie. "I knew about AA from something I'd read in a magazine a long time ago. I went to the telephone and called. The girl who later became my sponsor took me to a meeting. That was the beginning.

"I won't say it was easy when I first came to AA. I was mentally and physically sick. I resented AA; hated all of you, hated me most of all. But I had no place else to go, so I kept coming to meetings until what you were trying to tell me began to sink in.

"I found out a lot of things. First, that alcoholism is a sickness. We can't be cured—but we can recover. I learned that the *first* drink is the one that gets me drunk; that one drink is too much and a thousand not enough. I found out that it isn't how much you drink or what you drink that counts; it's what drinking *does* to you. I found out that if drinking interferes with any area of your life, you can be pretty sure you're an alcoholic. They told me that I don't have to worry about not drinking for the rest of my life; I just don't drink today, *now*, one day at a time. I found out I don't have to drink if I don't want to. I have a choice. For the past ten months and one week, I've chosen not to drink.

"Today I have a place to go, friends who understand me because they've been there, too. I come to meetings because I want to, not because I have to. AA has become my way of life. Sure, I still have problems, but I can face them sober, a day at a time. I find it unnecessary to drink—no matter what."

Nathalie smiled broadly. "And if I can do it, anyone can," she said. "To the new people, let me say, keep coming back. Take phone numbers, talk to us after the meeting. There isn't anyone in the room who won't be glad and even grateful to you for letting him help you. Carrying the message of AA is one of the ways we stay sober ourselves. So help us by helping yourself."

After the applause died down, there were announcements about upcoming parties, picnics, and conferences.

Then everyone joined hands and said the Lord's Prayer.

Jim slipped a piece of paper into Davy's hand. "My phone number," he said. "The first week was the hardest for me. I had to call my sponsor twenty times a day. Call me, Davy, anytime. We'll talk."

Davy stuffed the paper into his pocket. "Thanks," he said. He couldn't see himself calling a perfect stranger and crying on his shoulder.

"Let me tell you something," said Jim. "Nobody's too dumb to make the program, but a lot of people are too smart. Think it over." He clapped Davy on the shoulder. "I've got to help clean up," he said. "See you around."

Davy looked around for Maxi. She was surrounded by Tina and some other girls. He waited for her to finish talking, then they headed for the door.

"Tina's going to call me," said Maxi. "She wants to meet me at another meeting tomorrow night."

"That's great," said Davy. He wasn't sure about AA. All these people sounded so . . . well . . . so good; too good to be true. They were probably all a bunch of phonies, but he didn't want to discourage Maxi.

"Rochelle took my phone number, too," said

Maxi. "Oh, Davy, they're all just like us. They *know* how it is. And if they could stop drinking, so can we." She looked at him, her eyes sparkling. "Oh, Davy, do you think we have a chance?"

"Sure," said Davy. "Why not?"

But deep inside he had his doubts.

8

Davy and Maxi went to AA meetings every night for the next several days. Maxi took in everything she heard at the meetings. She read the AA book and all the literature she could get. She made Tina her guru and telephoned her several times a day, despite the warning to take her time finding a sponsor. She began to spout AA slogans and philosophy. She was on a kind of high.

Davy had never seen her that way before. Although she had been told to take it easy, to try not to swallow the whole program at once, she had taken to AA with a passion. She was on what they called a "honeymoon," and she and Davy saw no one except for AA people.

It was not the same for Davy. He could not accept the program on blind faith. He had to analyze it and pick it apart. He questioned everything Jim said. And he argued until Jim, almost out of patience with him, said, "Don't analyze, just utilize. The program works, why fight it?"

Davy's feelings were mixed. He was glad to see Maxi happy. And he had to admit to himself that he felt better, too. He was no longer winded to the point of puking when he jogged around the track; his schoolwork began to make sense to him—he even found himself making real conversaton with his mother. Mostly, he was grateful. There were hours at a time when he didn't so much as think of booze.

But he began to resent the influence the group had over Maxi. He also began to resent his own presence at meetings. From the beginning, he came to the meetings for Maxi's sake. But *he* didn't need any group; he was not an alcoholic. He could take the stuff or leave it. Wasn't he proving that right now by not drinking?

Davy began to feel isolated, depressed; and he didn't know why.

"Did you ever see such a perfect day?" said Maxi to Davy as they drove away from the school one bright, sunshiny Friday afternoon. "It's a shame to go home."

"Yeah," said Davy.

"We should do something," said Maxi.

"What have you got in mind?"

"Something fun. Something outside." She paused. "I know. A picnic, we'll have a picnic."

"Now?"

"Sure, now. I'll drive by my house, throw some stuff together, and we'll go to the hideout, okay?"

Davy looked at her. If a person could sparkle, then Maxi was sparkling. Her eyes shining, she was radiant like the sunshine; bright and warm. "Okay by me," he said, not really interested but wanting to please her.

Maxi switched on the radio and began to hum. "Come on, Davy, sing," she said. "Get with it."

Davy half smiled and waved her suggestion away. All the way home, Maxi, beaming, cheerily sang along with the radio.

She parked in front of her house, went in, and a couple of minutes later she came out lugging a picnic basket on one arm and a blanket in the other.

Driving toward the park. Davy felt listless. He was bored but he didn't want to spoil Maxi's good time.

Davy carried the basket down the wash while Maxi spread the blanket. "What's to eat?" he asked, pretending to be interested.

"A real feast," said Maxi. "Half a baked chicken, three hard rolls—or stale—I don't know. Just unload the stuff, you'll see."

Davy got on his knees and pulled two Cokes

out of the basket and laid them on the blanket. "Got an opener?"

"Keep unloading, you'll come to it."

He emptied the basket and found the opener. He also found something else. Hidden under the newspaper that covered the bottom was a bottle of booze. "Hey, what's this?" Davy asked, holding it up.

"How'd that get in there?" said Maxi, coming over to look.

"Must be left over from the good old days," said Davy.

"Yeah," said Maxi. "Well, just throw it away."

"Throw it away?"

Maxi looked at him.

Davy didn't know what to say next. He was appalled at the idea of throwing perfectly good booze away. "Why don't we start with a drink?" he said light-heartedly.

"That's not funny."

"We can handle it. Hell, one drink won't hurt anything," said Davy, unscrewing the bottle cap.

"Stop it, Davy!"

He held the bottle up. The liquor shone amber in the sunlight. "Looks good," he said grinning.

"Stop it!" Maxi stood over him.

"Here's to you," Davy said as he raised the bottle up to his mouth.

Maxi snatched the bottle from his hands and flung it to the other side of the wash. It broke with a crash.

They looked at each other silently. Then: "What's the matter with you?" said Davy.

"*Me?* What's the matter with *me?*"

"I was only joking," Davy said. "Can't you take a joke?"

"Yeah, some joke! You were going to drink it!"

"I was only kidding!"

"Sure you were," said Maxi sarcastically.

Davy shook his head. "Boy, ever since you got on AA you've been out of it!"

"I suppose you liked us better drunk!"

"What are you talking about?" said Davy.

"Did you like us better the way we used to be? Sloshing around in our own vomit . . . out of it most of the time . . . sneaking around, doing anything for a drink . . . anything . . ."

Davy interrupted. "If you want to know the truth," he lashed back, "that wasn't so bad! At least we had some fun once in a while!"

Maxi broke into tears and turned away. Davy was sorry. He hadn't meant to make her cry. He touched her arm but she pulled away.

"Aw, come on, Maxi . . ."

"Go away . . . get out of here," said Maxi.

"I'm sorry, Maxi . . . please . . ."

"Get out . . . get out of here," she said.

"Okay, okay, if that's the way you want it!" Davy turned and climbed up the incline.

He was full of anger toward Maxi as he headed home. His best friend, and that's how well she knew him! She couldn't even tell when he was fooling around. Hell, he was nowhere near drinking the stuff.

Then another thought took hold.

Suppose she hadn't stopped him? Would he have taken the drink? He didn't know. He honestly didn't know.

Now, he felt sorry, ashamed. He had no right to tease Maxi like that.

But by the time he got home he was angry again, convinced he was right and she was wrong. She was no fun anymore, had no sense of humor. And who was she to tell him what to do anyway? If he wanted to drink, he good and well would. She couldn't stop him.

He went into the den and poured himself a glass of scotch. He looked at it for a moment. If he drank it, she would have won the argument. Suddenly he poured it back into the bottle. Hell, if Maxi could stay sober, so could he.

Davy came late to the AA meeting that night. The kids were sitting around the table, ready to start a participation meeting. He looked around for Maxi. But when she caught his eye, he pretended not to see her. Her face clouded as she turned to talk to Tina. Davy sat down on the opposite side of the table.

Rochelle opened the meeting. "I see a few newcomers here and I'd like you to know what AA is and what it isn't," she said. "AA is a group of people who share their experience, strength, and hope with each other to solve their common problems and try to help other people recover, too."

Not again, thought Davy. I've heard all this before. Why do they have to be so repetitious?

Rochelle went on: "It is not a prohibitionist, philantropic, or religious group. The only requirement for membership is a desire to stop drinking. Tonight, we're having a problem discussion meeting. Anybody got a problem, or something they want to share?"

There was silence while Rochelle looked around the table. "So everybody's happy ...nobody has a problem ... terrific!"

The group laughed. Davy scanned their faces. They all seemed so relaxed, calm. He felt like bashing their serene faces in, but he had to admit grudgingly to himself that they really looked happy.

A girl held up her hand. "Yes. Penny," said Rochelle.

Penny spoke almost in a whisper. "I've been invited to a party," she said. "And I know there's going to be drinking there. I'm scared. I've only been sober for two weeks."

Rochelle called on another girl to answer Penny. "My name is Jody," said the girl, "and I'm also an alcoholic. I don't know if this is going to help, but I'll share it anyway. The other night I went to a party and most of the kids were drinking. Well, I just put some ginger ale in my glass, and you know what? Nobody even noticed whether I was drinking or not—they were only interested in what they were drinking, themselves. I always thought I'd have a rotten time at a party if I wasn't drinking, but I had a great time." Jody laughed. "Besides, the next day I didn't have a hangover and I remembered everything that happened. I even went water-skiing."

"That's one way of handling it," said Rochelle. "I had to do it differently. I was too scared to go to parties where there was drinking going on when I was new. I didn't know how to refuse a drink, so I just plain stayed away from drinkers. For me, that was okay—that's the way I had to do it. Now, I still stick pretty close to other AA's. I feel more comfortable and have a better time." She paused. "Believe me, I wouldn't trade the best day I had drinking for the worst I've had sober."

Davy shifted in his seat. He was getting bored.

Rochelle nodded to a boy who raised his hand.

"My name is Robert," said the boy. "I'm new

here and I don't know whether I'm an alcoholic or just a heavy drinker. How can I be sure?"

"Who wants to answer that?" said Rochelle.

Jim took the floor. "There's a pamphlet here called 'Twenty Questions,' and if you can answer 'yes' to any of them, chances are you are an alcoholic. But what I've heard around these meetings is that hardly anyone ever comes to AA by mistake. If you're worried about your drinking, you probably have a problem. But you have to decide that for yourself. No one can tell anyone else if he is or isn't."

Well, that lets me out, thought Davy. I've quit drinking and have no big problems, so what am *I* doing here?

"But I only drink beer or wine, never the hard stuff," said Robert.

Tina responded: "We found out that no matter how the drink is flavored, the *alcohol* that's in it can get us just as drunk as the hard stuff." Tina paused. "There's one other thing: nobody can force you to drink, just as nobody else can get you sober. It's a do-it-yourself program. I used to think I drank because my parents wouldn't shape up, because all my friends drank . . . I had a hundred reasons for drinking. But I found out that nobody bent my elbow for me—I did it all by myself."

Maxi was hanging on Tina's words, looking at her worshipfully. A feeling of resentment swept over Davy. He'd had enough. He was tired of all the talk, all the goody-goody stuff.

Without quite knowing what made him so angry, he got up and left the room.

9

It was Maxi who ended the freeze. She telephoned Davy at home. He was glad to hear from her, and they began to meet again. But in all of their meetings after that they never mentioned the scene at the wash. Both seemed glad to avoid the subject. And while they were happy to be together again, it was different. They weren't as easy with each other anymore. The old comfortable feeling between them was gone. They found themselves being polite, even guarded.

Davy wondered about their relationship. He loved her, but he missed the old Maxi, the crazy, loving, affectionate Maxi. He longed for the closeness they used to have, the feeling of both of them against the world.

Davy began to skip meetings. He kept making up excuses for Maxi—either he had homework to do, or his dad was home and wanted him around the house . . . whatever.

It bothered him to have to lie to Maxi, but he told himself he was doing it for her. He didn't want her to get turned off on AA. There was nothing wrong with the program if a person needed it. And Maxi needed it.

But he didn't. The complusion to drink had left him—the old craving for booze was gone.

Saturday night, as Davy walked to Maxi's house, he had a strange, restless feeling. He wanted to do something exciting, different . . . break loose. He chuckled to himself. It must be the weather, spring fever or something. Well, maybe he and Maxi could go get a hamburger, then drive to Disneyland . . . or they could go down to the beach. Maxi might go for that.

As he walked up the driveway Davy could smell the scent of good food cooking in the camper. "Come on in," called Maxi when he knocked.

Maxi, grinning, stood in front of the little table. She stepped aside. The table was set with colorful dishes and a birthday cake with one candle in the center. "Surprise!" she sang out. "Happy birthday!"

"What's all this?" said Davy. "My birthday's in December."

"It's *our* birthday," smiled Maxi. "It's been a whole month since either of us had a drink. Isn't it super?"

Her high spirits annoyed him slightly. "Yeah, sure," said Davy.

"I cooked us a far-out dinner to celebrate."

"Great," said Davy.

Maxi was disappointed. "You don't sound too thrilled," she said.

Davy didn't want her to be hurt. "I thought we'd do something special tonight, go someplace."

"We will," said Maxi. "After dinner we can go to the clubhouse. Tina said there'd be a good speaker."

Davy couldn't help himself. That was the last thing he felt like doing. He held up his index finger and described circles in the air. "Oh, wow," he said scornfully.

"Well, sit down," said Maxi. "We can't let all this good stuff go to waste."

The two ate in chilly silence and when they were finished, Maxi cleared up. The cake remained on the table untouched.

"Want some cake?" said Maxi.

"Okay," Davy said.

Maxi lit the candle on the cake. "We earned this," she said softly. "Happy birthday, Davy."

"Big deal," said Davy. "So we stopped drinking for a month. Who needs all these dumb games?"

Maxi stiffened. "It's not dumb. It's important. Probably the most important thing in our lives."

"Okay, okay," said Davy. "It's important. I just don't dig playing all these weird kid games."

Without speaking, they finished their cake. "I take it you don't want to go to a meeting?" said Maxi.

"How'd you guess?"

Maxi looked at him. Then she smiled. "Well," she said, "I guess I could skip a meeting just this once. Want to go to a movie? The Fox has a good one on."

"Uh, uh," said Davy. "Not in the mood."

"Whatever mood you are in, it's rotten," Maxi said. "What *do* you feel like doing?"

"I don't know. Maybe go for a ride."

"A ride, where?"

"Anywhere. Too nice to be inside. The beach, maybe."

Maxi sighed. "Okay," she said.

"Malibu?" said Maxi, driving toward the beach road.

Vista Beach was where all the kids hung out. "No, let's go to Vista. See if there's any action."

"I thought we'd go to Malibu. There's such a beautiful moon. We could sit and talk," said Maxi.

Sure, and listen to her yak about AA and all that garbage, thought Davy. "Come on, let's see what's doing at Vista," he urged.

Davy saw Maxi hesitate. "We can go to Malibu later," he said.

"Fair enough," said Maxi, heading toward Vista Beach.

They parked behind the snack stand and walked down toward the water. The moon was so bright it was almost like daylight. A girl Scout troop was having a wiener roast around a fire-ring near the water's edge. Maxi and Davy walked along the beach passing groups of picnickers, couples lying close on blankets, joggers, and strollers.

They found a clear place and laid their blanket down. Transistor rock music, almost drowning out the sound of the ocean, wafted over them as they took off their shoes and threw them onto the blanket. Maxi took Davy's hand and looked out over the water. "Nice," she said.

Davy looked across the beach down the sand. Fire-rings, glowing yellow and red, dotted the beach. He was suddenly reminded of that New Year's Eve long ago when he felt as if he was the only one in the world not invited to a party. He pulled Maxi's hand. "Come on, let's walk," he said.

"Okay," said Maxi.

Hand in hand, they strolled down the beach. The sounds of music and laughter grew stronger as they approached a group around a fire-ring.

One of the boys separated himself from the

group. It was Cliff. "If it ain't the gruesome twosome," he laughed. "Hey, look who's here! It's Maxi and Davy!"

Linda, wearing a heavy sweat shirt over shorts, came running over. Mike followed her.

"Long time no see," said Mike. "How's it going?"

"Fine . . . terrific," said Davy guardedly. The last time he'd been with the gang was at Maxi's party, the night they stripped her. But now the kids seemed easy, friendly, as if that night had never happened.

"Come on," said Maxi to Davy. "Let's go."

Linda sidled up to Davy. "Why don't you stay?" she said. "I'll let you marsh my mallow."

"Sure," said Mike. "Join the crowd, we're having a blast."

"Sorry, we have to go," said Maxi.

"Oh, don't be a couple of droops, stick around for a while," said Linda.

Davy knew they should go. But he was perversely, inexplicably drawn toward them. He wanted to stay.

Maxi took Davy's arm. "Thanks for the invitation, but Davy and I are leaving," she said firmly.

Davy shot Maxi a look. She had no right coming off so bossy.

Maxi met his stare. "We have someplace else to go," she said, pulling him by the arm.

Davy shook her hand off. "We can stay for a while," he said.

"The place is here, the time is now," laughed Mike. He pulled Maxi along with him. "Sit down, baby, have something to drink."

"I don't drink anymore," said Maxi shortly. She flicked a pleading look at Davy.

What did she want from him? She was doing all right by herself, he thought, turning away.

Mike pulled Maxi down by the fire-ring. "Okay, okay, have a Coke. Give Maxi a Coke, someone."

Davy saw Maxi hesitate, then take the Coke. "We'll be leaving in a minute," she said thinly.

"Sit by me," said Linda, plunking herself down on her blanket. Davy looked at her. With the firelight on her face and the moonlight behind her she looked beautiful.

Someone turned up the volume on the transistor. Loud, blaring rock music filled the air. "Dance time!" said Mike, pulling Maxi to her feet. Davy watched while some of the group started dancing on the sand.

"Sit down," called Paul to Davy. "Take a load off your brains."

Linda reached up and pulled Davy down on the blanket. Then she looked across the fire at Paul. "You're so stupid, if your brains were gasoline, you couldn't drive a gocart around a pinhead," she laughed.

107

"Well, if your brains were TNT, you couldn't blow your nose," retorted Paul loudly.

Davy laughed along with the kids around the fire. He hadn't realized how much he'd missed being with them.

"Hungry? Want a dog?" asked Linda.

"No thanks," said Davy.

Linda put a paper cup into Davy's hands. She poured herself a drink, then filled Davy's cup. "Here's to us," she said, then tipped her cup.

Davy looked down at the cup in his hand. He glanced at Maxi, dancing with Mike. Her back was toward him. One drink wouldn't hurt anything. Hell, Maxi'd never know.

"To us," Davy said and swallowed the drink. He'd heard so much about the "evils of drinking" in the past month that he was almost surprised that he didn't self-destruct. He felt only a pleasant sense of well-being, a glowing warmth.

Cliff, sitting on the blanket beside him, broke out into song:

"The first verse, the same as the first,
The beer was on the wall,
The second verse, the same as the first,
The beer was on the wall . . ."

Other kids around the fire took up the refrain, overpowering the transistor radio:

"The third verse, the same as the first,
The beer was on the wall,
The fourth verse, the same as the first,
The beer was on the wall . . ."

Linda poured more booze into Davy's cup. He drank and linked arms with Linda, and sang along with the crowd:

"The fifth verse, the same as the first,
The beer was on the wall,
The sixth verse, the same as the first,
The beer was . . ."

Maxi was suddenly in front of him. "Let's go, Davy," she said. "It's getting late."

"Who's going anywhere? The party's just beginning!" said Mike, coming up behind Maxi and putting his arm around her.

Maxi shrugged his arm off. "We've got to go," she said. "Are you coming?" she asked Davy.

"What is she, your wife or something?" shouted Linda above the singing.

"We'll go soon," Davy said, embarrassed.

"We're going now," said Maxi stubbornly.

Davy tried to signal Maxi with his eyes, but she looked away. Why did she have to be such a turkey?

"Don't be a party-pooper," said Linda.

"What you need is a drink," said Mike, thrusting a paper cup into Maxi's hand.

"No," said Maxi.

"It's only a Coke, for God's sake," Mike said.

Why can't she see she's coming off like a bitch, thought Davy.

"If you want to leave, go," said Linda. "Davy's staying, aren't you, Davy?"

"Yeah," said Davy. "I'm staying."

Maxi looked at Davy.

Mike took a long drink from his cup and put his arm around Maxi again. "Come on, Maxi baby, we were dancing, remember?"

Maxi ignored Mike. "Davy?" she said.

The drinks were having their effect. Davy felt ten feet tall, in command. "I'm staying," he said. "Why don't you relax and have a good time?"

Maxi stared at him.

"Drink up, Maxi, we're all ahead of you," said Linda. "Don't be so uncool."

Davy could see Maxi's confusion. It made him uncomfortable. But the good sport in her won out. Looking at him, she raised her cup to him and drank. Davy was relieved.

Maxi turned to Mike. "Hey, what did you put in this Coke?"

"Who, me?" said Mike in mock innocence.

"It's booze . . . you put booze in my Coke!" sputtered Maxi. "He spiked my drink!" she said to Davy.

Davy shrugged. "What the hell, you didn't explode or anything, did you?"

"Afraid you won't get to heaven?" teased Linda. She poured Davy another drink and put her arm around his shoulders.

For a moment Davy hesitated, then he drank up. "Look, Ma, I'm drinking, and I didn't even drop dead," he said.

Maxi stared at him while the others laughed. Davy looked back at her defiantly. He saw shock in her eyes. Was it anger? Fear? He didn't know. He didn't care. He felt too good.

At last, Maxi looked away. She held up her drink. "Happy days," she said and finished it off.

Davy watched Mike lead Maxi to the group dancing on the sand. He felt free, as if a load had been lifted from him. He turned to Linda. "How about a little more of that firewater?" he said.

The evening grew noisier, wilder. Cliff and his girl took off with their blanket to a more secluded part of the beach. The couples dancing clung to each other. Davy's vision was blurring. He was beginning to see everything through a drunken screen.

A couple of the guys were throwing Frisbees over the heads of the dancers.

"Knock it off," a girl yelled.

"Take it off!" someone shouted.

The girl pulled off her T-shirt. Everyone stopped dancing. The gang howled and

111

clapped as she did a burlesque dance. Davy joined in the applause as they egged her on.

Exhausted and naked, the girl fell to the sand.

Davy took Linda's bottle and gulped. He could feel her at his side cuddling closer.

"How about skinny-dipping?" shouted Mike.

"Off with your clothes, everyone!" yelled Mike.

"Take it off! Take it off!" the gang cried.

Davy shook his head trying to clear his vision. He seemed able to see only one element at a time. He moved his head to look from one scene to another. Here, a group stood naked, laughing and talking about who goes into the water first. There, whooping and hollering, a parade of images danced crazily around the fire-ring, Indian-style.

Davy wanted to participate in the fun. He got up, swayed dizzily, and sat back down. He felt frustrated. His drinks had never hit him this fast before. He hadn't meant to get this drunk.

He turned to Linda. Slack-jawed, he watched her strip beside him. Suddenly, she put her arms around him and kissed him full on the lips.

When they came out of their clinch, Maxi was standing before them stripped down to her panties. She weaved drunkenly for a moment, then she took both of Davy's hands and tried to pull him up. He sat like marble, unable to move.

Maxi dropped Davy's hands. "Going skinny-dipping . . . out for a swim," she giggled. "You coming or not?"

Davy wanted to go. But his legs felt like lead. He was paralyzed. He clutched the bottle to his chest. "Not me," he mumbled. "You guys go ahead."

"You're nothing but a baby . . . a bottle baby," said Linda as she stood up and ran toward the water's edge.

"Let's go, Maxi!" he heard Mike yell.

Then for an instant, his eyes held on Maxi's. He had a momentary flash: Maxi's drunk!

But his thoughts were shattered as Maxi turned and, holding Mike's hand, ran into the surf.

Davy raised the bottle to his lips. He could feel the liquid dribbling out of the sides of his mouth. Then he lay down on the blanket. He could hear shouts and laughter. They grew fainter and fainter.

He passed out, dead drunk.

10

A shrill scream awakened Davy. The sound seemed to come from a long way off.

Davy raised himself on an elbow and turned his head toward the sound. Other voices joined the first one but Davy could hear only anxious, disjointed phrases: "What happened . . . hurry . . . Oh my God . . ."

Davy tried to focus his eyes. In the bright moonlight he could make out the figure of a boy. Was it Mike? Davy squinted. He couldn't quite tell. The boy was carrying a limp body in his arms. A sense of alarm gripped Davy. He tried to get up but couldn't. He looked again.

Other kids came running. He heard the sound of girls crying, whimpering, then Mike's voice ordering: "Get the head back . . . mouth to mouth . . ."

Davy moved aside as someone stumbled over him. The fire had burned out and he could see shadowy figures of kids dressing hurriedly. They were making small, frightened, animal sounds. He wanted to ask what was going on, but he couldn't form the words. His head was whirling. He closed his eyes and saw flashes of swiftly changing colors. He was dreaming ... one of those nightmares ...

Davy opened his eyes again at the eerie scream of an ambulance. Strong lights were playing over the water, on the sand. The white hulk of the ambulance halted by the circle of kids. A hush fell over them as they stood watching the attendants.

Davy wanted to find out who was hurt. But he couldn't get his legs to work. He lay helplessly out of control.

Suddenly, he heard a shriek. "Oh no! No, no, no ... oh, Maxi, Maxi ..."

Other voices, crying out, sobbing. One saying, "It can't be ... she was such a good swimmer ... dead ... she's dead ..."

Coming out of nowhere, a small, cold clod of fear started in Davy's stomach, then surged up and spread to the tips of his limbs, leaving him weak and sweating.

Forcing himself to look back down at the beach, he saw the circle of kids open to let the attendants carry a covered body on a stretcher to the ambulance door, where the stretcher disappeared into darkness.

Davy rolled over on his back and looked up at the sky. He was sure he would wake up in a

115

minute, sure that what he had experienced was only a dream, one of the bad ones.

He heard cars starting in the distance. A dream . . . only a dream. He closed his eyes and slept.

Davy was awakened by a dull prodding. Cliff and a girl were trying to rouse him. Their voices seemed to come to him from behind a heavy black curtain:

"Let's get him to the car," Cliff said.

"He won't budge, let's go," said the girl.

"If the cops find him drunk, he'll be busted," said Cliff. "Come on, give me a hand."

The girl started crying. "No, please, take me home. If my folks knew I was here. I'd get killed."

"Grab his other arm."

Davy tried to talk, to tell them something, but he couldn't get the words out. He felt himself being dragged over the sand by his arms. He groaned. It felt as if his arms were being torn off at the sockets. He could hear Cliff and the girl grunting as they pulled him along.

"Cliff, the cops! They're coming this way!" the girl suddenly said. "Dump him . . . let's split!"

"Okay, come on!" Cliff said.

Davy felt himself being dropped in the sand. It became quiet and he sank back into sleep.

Davy awakened to the hot sun beating down on him. He sat up and looked around. The smooth ocean shimmered, the bright sun hurt his eyes. His vision blurred, then cleared, then blurred again. Suddenly, he started to retch but nothing came up. Spasms of dry heaves racked his body.

Weakly, he stood up. His heart palpitating, he walked to the surf and ducked his head into the cool water. As he walked out of the water he remembered an image of someone else coming out of the water, carrying a body. Ah yes, now he knew what it was. It was a dream. He had had a terrible nightmare, but he couldn't remember any details.

He tried to recall last night's events. Why had the gang left him on the beach alone? Had something happened? What? His stomach tightened with anxiety. Where was Maxi? Why should she leave him? He remembered something . . . something vaguely about skinny-dipping. Maxi had been giggling . . . drinking . . . Maxi had been drunk! Had she gotten so drunk she had forgotten him? He tried, but couldn't remember any more. Well, he'd find out when he got home. But there was something frightening niggling at the back of his mind.

He would think about that later. What faced him now was the thought of going home after being out all night. That would be one hell of a scene. He was feeling rotten; he seemed to ache all over. Coffee. He'd get some coffee, then go home and get it over with.

The counter man and an elderly woman were so engrossed in conversation they didn't hear Davy come into the snack stand. He sat at the counter and waited.

". . . the way kids nowadays carry on. Something ought to be done about it . . . ruining our property . . . spoiling the beach. It's a wonder there hasn't been a tragedy before this."

Davy thought of the image that had been eluding him . . . the nightmare. He listened nervously.

"I'm with you," said the counter man. "I hate to see a young girl drown, but it's like they ask for it."

The horror of the night suddenly came back to him. Davy could hear the shriek, shrill and penetrating. It wasn't a dream. It had all happened! In one terrible instant Davy knew the truth. Maxi was dead! Oh, no, no, no . . . oh, Maxi, Maxi . . .

He stood up, his head reeling. His knees buckled and he held onto the counter to keep from falling.

"Hey, kid," said the counter man. "Something wrong? You sick or something?"

Davy looked at him, then started out the door.

"Probably strung out on something," he could hear the man say as he left.

Davy ran wildly to the highway and tried to hitch a ride. His mind was a blank. He felt nothing. Through a blur, he could see cars going and coming. When, a while later, a pickup truck stopped for him, he could only stare at the driver.

"Well, you want a lift or not?" said the driver.

Davy nodded.

"Hop in back and let's get going," the driver said.

Davy got into the truckbed and sat next to a huge black dog. When the truck started, the dog moved close to him and licked his face. Davy buried his face in the animal's coat and held him tightly. Then the dog moved out of his embrace and sat looking at him, sad-eyed.

The question that had been nagging at him sprang to mind. Now, he remembered why he had been left at the beach alone all night.

The truck took an onramp onto the freeway and picked up speed. Davy thought of Maxi. He saw her struggling in the water, gasping for air.

"Oh my God," he thought, "Maxi's dead!"

It wasn't true, it couldn't be. But it was. Maxi was dead . . . she was dead! He pounded his fist on the truckbed until his knuckles bled.

Now his thoughts crowded in on each other.

If anyone had to die, why wasn't it him? He was the bastard. What happened was his fault. She hadn't wanted to go to the beach. She had wanted to go to a meeting. Why hadn't he listened to her? He made her go. He killed her. He was the one who deserved to die. He ought to kill himself.

Why not? He could do it right now. He edged closer to the end of the truck. He could jump out of the speeding truck and it would all be over in a minute.

Dangling his legs over the edge of the truck, he looked down at the racing roadway beneath him. A large trailer was following a short distance behind. He leaned forward. Both hands clutched the edge of the truck.

Then the dog came over and licked his face. Davy straightened. He couldn't do it . . . he couldn't. A wave of self-loathing came over him. He was too damned cowardly to kill himself even when all he wanted to do was die.

Davy's father was waiting for him at the door. Davy wanted to cry, to tell his father what had happened, but he didn't have a chance. His father grabbed him around the neck.

"There are certain rules we have around this household, in case you haven't noticed!" he yelled.

Davy tried to free himself but his father wouldn't let go.

"Your mother's been up all night worrying about you! But not me! I don't worry about you anymore! You don't give a good damn about us, why should I be concerned about you!"

Davy couldn't find his voice to speak. Maxi was dead and all his father could think about was his being out all night.

Enraged, his father let go of him. "Why don't you shape up . . . pull yourself together? Look at you! You look like a derelict, a bum!"

Martha came and stood beside Frank. She was crying. "Oh, Davy, Davy. What are we going to do with you?"

Davy couldn't stand the sight of his mother crying. He looked away. "I'm all right," he made himself say.

Suddenly, he was seized with a violent cramp, and grabbed his stomach with both hands.

"Frank, he's sick!" said Martha. "Put him to bed!"

"I've gotta . . . go . . . to . . . the bathroom," Davy managed to breathe.

"I'm not through with him yet!" exploded Frank. "He's a disgrace! We ought to have him declared incorrigible—have him made a ward of the court! Lord knows, we've done everything we could!"

Davy's stomach churned. He had to get to the bathroom urgently. "Lemme go!" he said.

His father held him fast by the shoulder. "I'm talking to you! I'll have a little respect while I'm talking!"

Suddenly Davy's bowels turned to water and he felt a hot stream gush down his leg. He lurched out of his father's grasp and ran to the bathroom and locked the door. There he took off his pants, rinsed them out, and hung them over the towel bar to dry. Then he washed up and went to his room, a towel wrapped around his waist.

His parents were waiting for him. "This is the last straw!" Frank bellowed.

"Wait, let me," said Martha. "Davy, we're thinking of putting you into the hospital . . . you're sick . . . you're . . ."

"Stop walking on eggs!" yelled Frank. "Tell him like it is! What we decided is that we're taking you to Camarillo. We're having you locked up."

Davy froze. He stared at his father. Something exploded inside him; like a rocket starting at his toes and swelling to blow out of his head. He had to hit back, do something. Maxi was dead! He tried to scream but nothing came out. Crazed, he picked up a lamp and threw it against the mirror over the dresser. The glass shattered and fell out in pieces.

Martha screamed. Frank tried to hold him, but Davy fought him off.

Davy grabbed a baseball bat from the corner of his room and circled it menacingly around his head. Frank backed away.

"You're crazy . . . I'm calling the police!" said Frank. Taking Martha's arm, he pulled her out of the room.

Davy dropped the bat on the floor and dressed hurriedly. He had to get out of there. He'd get out and never come back . . . never!

He grabbed his wallet and ran toward the front door. He could hear his parents talking in their bedroom. He passed the kitchen, then stopped and went back. He took his mother's car keys and ran out the front door.

He got into his mother's car and backed it out of the driveway. Tires squealing, he shot up the street. He had no idea of where he was heading, he just had to go . . . fast. Another car blasted its horn as he raced past a stop sign. Passing a car ahead of him, he swerved, barely missing it. He barreled down Woodman Avenue, ignoring stop signs and signal lights. A street sign caught his eyes: Magnolia Boulevard. He tried for a left turn, but he was going so fast the car skidded out of control. The wheel spun crazily in his hands as he tried to right the car. Grazing another car parked at the curb, he turned the wheel sharply, jumped the opposite curb, went through a redwood fence onto a lawn, and crashed into a tree.

For a moment, Davy sat stunned. Then, unhurt, he opened the car door and ran. Taking side streets and cutting through yards, he made his way to a parallel avenue. He ran until cramps forced him to slow down. Then he saw a bike leaning against a tree in front of a house. He got on the bike and rode away. He could hear the sound of a police siren in the distance.

Pumping as hard as he could, he rode on until he came within two blocks of the park. He left the bike between two parked cars and ran the rest of the way.

At last at the wash, he stumbled down the incline and lay panting on the cement floor. The horrors of the last twenty-four hours washed over him once more.

"Maxi . . . Maxi," he cried again and again, convulsed with tears.

11

Davy didn't go to Maxi's funeral. He saw an article in the newspaper about her, and tore out the clipping and stuck it in his pocket.

The wash became his home. Day after day he sat there, leaving only to get more booze or something to eat. He knew vaguely that school had ended for the summer. When he thought of it at all, he knew his parents were probably looking for him. But he didn't care. His only concern was for booze. And to stay out of the way of the cops.

When he wasn't too drunk to see, he took the clipping out of his pocket, looked at Maxi's picture for a long time, then read the article again. "A tragic accident," was the way the paper put it. That phrase always got to him. He felt her death was no "accident." He felt as if he had taken a gun and shot her. That was always the occasion for another drink.

He got by fairly easily for as long as his money lasted. When the money ran out, he began to mooch booze from the other drunks. Then when he couldn't pay it back, the old boozers in the park avoided him. He was alone as he had never been before. He began to beg. If he couldn't get money that way, he stole.

At night, he went back to the wash to sleep. He rarely fell into a natural sleep—he passed out. Amid wild, frightening nightmares, kicking with his arms and legs, he'd wake up dehydrated. He drank volumes of water in the rest room. But no matter how much he drank, he was still thirsty.

Each morning, although he washed up, the smell of stale whiskey seemed to ooze out of his pores.

Again and again, sitting in the wash, Davy went over the night of Maxi's death in his mind. All along, he had felt responsible; guilty and ashamed. But now he remembered Mike. Mike had spiked Maxi's drink. *He* was responsible for her death. Davy decided to go and find Mike. The rage he felt motivated him, gave him a purpose for the first time in days. He'd find Mike and let him have it. He'd beat him to a bloody pulp. He'd cripple him!

He climbed out of the wash and walked to Mike's house. Mike's blue van was parked in front. That meant he was at home. Davy sat down on the curb to wait. Mike had to come out sometime. Pounding his fist into the palm of his hand, Davy pictured himself cracking Mike on the jaw, pummeling him, beating him.

Suddenly, Mike was standing over him. "What do *you* want? What are you doing here?"

Davy stood up waveringly. He grabbed Mike's arm. "It's your fault . . . you killed her," he said.

Mike pulled his arm away and backed up. "You stinking son-of-a-bitch, what're you talking about?"

"Maxi . . . it's your fault . . . you killed her!" Davy swung wildly but mike stepped back out of reach.

"Crazy bastard, you're drunk!" Mike said.

Davy lunged, but again Mike sidestepped him. "Go home," he said, "I'm warning you."

Davy looked at Mike with hatred. He swung, brushing Mike's jaw. Mike smacked him hard in the face and pushed him on the ground. He stood over him looking down at Davy with contempt.

Then Mike got into the van and started the motor. "If I ever catch you around here again, I'll break both your legs!" he said out the window.

The van grazed Davy's leg as it took off and sped down the street.

Davy limped back to the park. He was bruised, dirty; he stank. He slept for a while.

When he woke, he decided not to spend another night in the park. He would wash up, then go away, leave town. He'd get a job, start a new life someplace else.

He went into the rest room and cleaned up as best he could. Looking up, he caught two images of himself in the mirror. There were dark hollows under each set of eyes. Stepping back, he held a hand over one eye and found he could focus. But as soon as he took his hand away, the double vision returned.

He splashed cold water over his face. Then he cupped his hands and drank. He couldn't get enough water. The moment he stopped drinking, his mouth was dry again.

He looked in the mirror once more. This time he saw a clear vision of himself. He needed fresh clothes and some money. And a drink. He had to have a drink. If he wanted to leave, he'd have to go home and get what he needed.

Davy left the rest room and started walking back to the house. How long had it been since he left? Was it days? Weeks? He couldn't remember.

When he reached home, he saw his mother's car in the driveway. He hid in back of the garage until she took the car and left. Then he went into the house and made straight for the den. He drank greedily, thirstily.

In his own room, he changed clothes, then went into his mother's room and took the money she kept hidden under the paper lining in her top dresser drawer. A piece of paper caught his eye on top of the dresser. It was the name and telephone number of the Van Nuys police station. They must still be looking for him. He thought of his mother. Was she worried about him? Naw, all his parents wanted to do was lock him up. He'd better get out fast. He put the money in his wallet and left the house.

Davy found himself walking toward Maxi's place. He had to see the camper just once more. He had to be where Maxi had been, touch what she had touched. Then, maybe, he could forget her, once and for all. On the way, he thought of her. Engulfed by sadness, his eyes filled with tears. The pain of his loss tore at him as if it happened today. He remembered the night he'd held her in his arms in front of the fire; the day they sat in the wash looking up at the clouds and laughing, the time she first took him to her hideaway.

When he reached her house, his heart sank at the sight of the Camaro, sitting forlorn and empty in the driveway. He hurried by it and tried the camper door.

"What do you think you're doing?"

Davy turned. Maxi's father had come up behind him. He was staring at him suspiciously.

"Nothing, I only . . ."

"Aren't you the kid that used to be hanging around here all the time?"

Davy nodded. The man looked mean and ugly. Davy felt a tightening in his chest, a kind of hatred for this man, as he remembered the time he had beaten Maxi up.

Davy turned to go but the man stepped closer.

"You're the punk that used to be sneaking around after I went to work! Don't think I don't know what was going on . . . you little shitheel! I ought to break your neck!"

"You got it all wrong . . . I loved her," said Davy.

"Loved her! What's a little fart like you know about love?" The man grabbed Davy's shoulder. "You played around with her, got her drunk! A lot you cared!" Then he swung and hit Davy a walloping blow on the jaw.

Davy fell to his knees.

"Get off this property, and don't let me ever see you here again or I swear I'll kill you!" The man turned and went into the house.

Davy stumbled down the street, then ducked into an alley. Trembling with rage, he reviewed his plans. He was leaving, that much was for sure! But first he had to have a drink. Feeling the sweat pour out of him, feeling shaky, he leaned against a wall. A strange buzzing sensation filled his head. He was sick. Sick, and maybe crazy. A nameless fear gripped him. He closed his eyes and felt himself sliding down the wall until he sank into a sitting position. One thing was certain: he was pretty far gone. He couldn't go on like this indefinitely. Maybe he ought to go home and let them lock him up. He shuddered at the thought.

He thought of AA and the halfway houses where they dried people up and helped them get back on their feet. Yeah, but who could live without drinking? He had tried that. It hadn't worked. Besides, he'd have to admit defeat, he'd have to surrender, as they said at AA. He'd have to reach his bottom. He pushed the thought out of his mind.

He'd go away from this town, start somewhere else, as he planned. Only first, he had to get some booze.

He opened his eyes and tried to get his bearings. There was a small liquor store not far from here. Holding onto the wall for support, he stood up and steadied himself.

Keeping to the back alleys as much as he could, Davy hurried to the store. He looked in the window and saw no customers inside. He would wait for a few people to come in. There'd be a better chance of his not being noticed if the place was busy.

As he stepped back, he was startled by the reflection of himself in the window. He looked haggard, shrunken, like the old winos who hung out in the park.

As he stood to the side waiting for the store to fill up, he felt someone pull at his arm. He looked down. A young boy was holding two wrinkled dollar bills in his fist.

"What do you want?" said Davy.

"Buy me some wine?" said the boy.

Davy looked at him. The kid was grinning, a cocky look on his face. A picture of himself flashed through Davy's mind. He saw himself a few years ago.

"What do you say? Will you do it?" said the boy.

"Get yourself a bottle of milk—with a nipple on it," said Davy angrily.

"Aw, come on," said the boy. "Do a kid a favor."

Suddenly, Davy exploded with anger. His fury was unreasoning. He wanted to hit the kid, smash him . . . kill him! He clenched his fists, trying to hold the rage down.

The boy waved the money in front of Davy's face. "Please . . . buy me some wine?"

Davy grabbed the kid by the collar.

"Lemme go . . . hey, lemme go . . ." the kid said, frightened.

Davy dug his fingers into the boy's shoulder. "Go home," he said between his teeth. "Go on home."

"Okay, lemme go . . . I'll go home . . . let go of me . . ." cried the boy. Then he gave a sudden lurch, twisted out of Davy's grasp, and ducked around the building.

Davy took off after him. He ran as fast as he could but the boy was too quick. The kid ducked into an alley and leaped over a wire fence, and by the time Davy hurdled it, the kid was out of sight. Davy thought his lungs were going to burst. He sat down exhausted, trying to catch his breath.

Suddenly he was crying. Hot tears streaming down his face, he put his head on his knees and sobbed. He didn't even try to stop himself. He was finished, done. He couldn't fight any longer. He couldn't think anymore. He could only hurt. He gave up . . . he surrendered. Davy didn't know how long he sat there crying.

"Oh God," he cried between sobs. "Oh God, help me!"

Davy got up and brushed himself off. He started walking. He knew where he had to go.

He felt empty, hollow, a stranger to himself as he approached the AA clubhouse.

A young guy met him at the door. He shook Davy's hand. "Hello," he said smiling. "I'm Gary."

"Hi," said Davy. "My name is Davy—I'm an alcoholic."

About the Author

In addition to writing books and educational material, Anne Snyder is active in the field of television. She is also a teacher of creative writing for gifted students at Valley College in North Hollywood and at Pierce College. Her book, FIRST STEP, was a winner of the 1976 Friends of American Writers Award. She and her husband live in Van Nuys, California.

SIGNET VISTA Books by John Neufeld

☐ **EDGAR ALLAN by John Neufeld.** In this penetrating novel, John Neufeld examines the problems that arise when a white middle class family adopts a black child. (#Y6628—$1.25)

☐ **LISA, BRIGHT AND DARK by John Neufeld.** Lisa is slowly going mad but her symptoms, even an attempted suicide, fail to alert her parents or teachers to her illness. She finds compassion only from three girlfriends who band together to provide what they call "group therapy." (#AE1189—$1.75)

☐ **FOR ALL THE WRONG REASONS by John Neufeld.** From the bestselling author of *Lisa, Bright and Dark* comes a tender, taut novel about a teenager marriage that speaks of today.
(#E9146—$1.75)

☐ **SUNDAY FATHER by John Neufeld.** The touching story of a young girl's painful adjustment to her parents' divorce. (#W7292—$1.50)

☐ **TWINK by John Neufeld.** The hopes, failures and courage of a young girl with cerebral palsy who could have been forgotten, and wasn't, and how love and touching and caring made the difference in the face of an almost overwhelming physical handicap.
(#W9145—$1.50)

Buy them at your local

bookstore or use coupon

on next page for ordering.

The Latest Books from SIGNET VISTA

Books from SIGNET VISTA

- ☐ A FIVE-COLOR BUICK AND A BLUE-EYED CAT by Phyllis Anderson Wood. (#AW1375—$1.50)
- ☐ I THINK THIS IS WHERE I CAME IN by Phyllis Anderson Wood. (#AW1482—$1.50)
- ☐ I'VE MISSED A SUNSET OR THREE by Phyllis Anderson Wood. (#Y7944—$1.25)
- ☐ SONG OF THE SHAGGY CANARY by Phyllis Anderson Wood. (#W9793—$1.50)
- ☐ WIN ME AND YOU LOSE by Phyllis Anderson Wood. (#Y8028—$1.25)
- ☐ YOUR BIRD IS HERE, TOM THOMPSON by Phyllis Anderson Wood. (#AW1001—$1.50)
- ☐ THE BETRAYAL OF BONNIE by Barbara Van Tuyl. (#W8879—$1.50)
- ☐ BONNIE AND THE HAUNTED FARM by Barbara Van Tuyl. (#AE1184—$1.75)
- ☐ A HORSE CALLED BONNIE by Pat Johnson and Barbara Van Tuyl. (#AE1184—$1.75)
- ☐ ELLEN GRAE AND LADY ELLEN by Vera and Bill Cleaver. (#J7832—$1.95)
- ☐ I WOULD RATHER BE A TURNIP by Vera and Bill Cleaver. (#W9539—$1.50)
- ☐ ME TOO by Vera and Bill Cleaver. (#Y6519—$1.25)
- ☐ GROVER by Vera and Bill Cleaver. (#AE1313—$1.95)
- ☐ THE WHYS AND WHEREFORES OF LITTABELLE LEE by Vera and Bill Cleaver. (#Y7225—$1.25)
- ☐ WHERE THE LILIES BLOOM by Vera and Bill Cleaver. (#AE1121—$1.75)

Buy them at your local

bookstore or use coupon

on next page for ordering.

SIGNET VISTA Books for Your Library

- [ ] **THE LIONHEARTED by Harriet Savitz.** (#Y7364—$1.75)
- [ ] **WAIT UNTIL TOMORROW by Harriet Savitz.** (#J9780—$1.95)
- [ ] **ADAM'S DAUGHTER by Gertrude Samuels.** (#AE1486—$1.75)
- [ ] **MOTTELE by Gertrude Samuels.** (#W7523—$1.50)
- [ ] **RUN, SHELLEY, RUN by Gertrude Samuels.** (#AE1443—$1.75)*
- [ ] **GET A LITTLE LOST, TIA by Phyllis Anderson Wood.** (#E9872—$1.75)
- [ ] **YOUR BIRD IS HERE, TOM THOMPSON by Phyllis Anderson Wood.** (#AW1001—$1.50)
- [ ] **WIN ME AND YOU LOSE by Phyllis Anderson Wood.** (#Y8028—$1.25)
- [ ] **FIVE WERE MISSING by Lois Duncan.** (#AE1040—$1.75)
- [ ] **DOWN A DARK HALL by Lois Duncan.** (#W9491—$1.50)
- [ ] **SYCAMORE YEAR by Mildred Lee.** (#AE1357—$1.75)*
- [ ] **FATHER FIGURE by Richard Peck.** (#J8846—$1.95)
- [ ] **NORTH TOWN by Lorenz Graham.** (#Y7624—$1.25)
- [ ] **SOUTH TOWN by Lorenz Graham.** (#AE1483—$1.75)

*Price slightly higher in Canada

Buy them at your local bookstore or use this convenient coupon for ordering.

THE NEW AMERICAN LIBRARY, INC.,
P.O. Box 999, Bergenfield, New Jersey 07621

Please send me the books I have checked above. I am enclosing $_____
(please add $1.00 to this order to cover postage and handling). Send check
or money order—no cash or C.O.D.'s. Prices and numbers are subject to change
without notice.

Name_____

Address_____

City _____ State _____ Zip Code _____

Allow 4-6 weeks for delivery.
This offer is subject to withdrawal without notice.